Myles Dillon, a distinguished Celticist, has taught at the University of Chicago and Edinburgh University. A former president of the Royal Irish Academy and author of numerous articles and books on Celtic studies, he is at present senior professor at the Dublin Institute for Advanced Studies.

THERE WAS A KING IN IRELAND

There was a king in Ireland...

FIVE TALES FROM ORAL TRADITION

Collected and Translated by

MYLES DILLON

ILLUSTRATED BY JOSÉ CISNEROS

PUBLISHED FOR THE *Texas Folklore Society* BY THE
UNIVERSITY OF TEXAS PRESS • AUSTIN & LONDON

International Standard Book Number 0-292-70138-1
Library of Congress Catalog Card Number 77-165912
© 1971 by Myles Dillon
All rights reserved
Printed by The University of Texas Printing Division, Austin
Bound by Universal Bookbindery, Inc., San Antonio

contents

7 Foreword

17 The Black Thief

37 The Queen of the Island of Loneliness

53 The Giant of the Mighty Blows

77 The Knowledge of the Only Story and the Dúdán's Sword

97 Terror without Fear

foreword

These stories were collected about forty years ago from Irish-speaking storytellers in County Galway. Only two have been published, one in Irish and another in an English translation, as explained hereafter. Most of them are already known in other versions, and I have given what information I could gather about each in turn. The special interest that attaches to this collection is that the translations exactly reproduce the original Irish, except where nonsense "runs" had to be rendered in alliterative form. And the original Irish is an exact record of what the speaker said, based upon dictaphone records, except for the last story, which was written down directly from the speaker's narrative. The book therefore gives a true account of oral tradition, such as is not to be found in Curtin or Larminie, or indeed, for that matter, in Grimm. The repeated formulae and the runs, which are essential features of the folktale and correspond to the formulae in Homer, are the very flavor of the story and are lost in any summary or "literary" retelling by an editor.

"The Black Thief" was published in volume 34 (1967) of Publications of the Texas Folklore Society. It had been our intention to publish the other tales in subsequent volumes, but the editor kindly suggested that the whole collection would make a little book of uniform character with a quality of its own, and this plan has been adopted.

The first four tales were recorded by dictaphone in September 1932 from Joe Flaherty ("Joe Mháirtin an tSagairt," Joe son of Martin, the Priest's Man), Ballycastle, Inisheer, Co. Galway. He was the best storyteller I ever met, and gesture and intonation added much to his performance. Even after the long interval of time I can still hear his voice in passages, when I read again. Fortunately some of these same tales were recorded from him twenty-six years later, and these later transcripts and mine are now in the archives of the Irish Folklore Commission and will provide valuable evidence about oral tradition.

The last tale, "Terror without Fear," was written without the aid of a dictaphone in April 1930 from the narration of Pat Gavan, Shruffane, Costelloe, Co. Galway. The Irish text was published in the *Zeitschrift für Celtische Philologie*, 19, pt. 2 (1932), 137-152, but the translation has not appeared before.

My thanks are due to my friend Seán Ó Súilleabháin for advice and help in preparing the notes on the first four tales, and to my friend Séamus Ó Duilearga for a summary of "Terror without Fear" following the Irish text in the *Zeitschrift*. To Wilson M. Hudson, editor for the Texas Folklore Society, I owe a special acknowledgment. The plan was his, and without his encouragement, amounting to insistence, I should never have disturbed these stories which have lain so long neglected. But his part in the book has been greater

Foreword 9

than that. He has prepared the manuscript for the press, commissioned the illustrations, consulted in the design, and assisted in reading proofs, and he is its patron and sponsor. This introduction might properly have been written by him, but he has preferred that I write it myself.

The Black Thief

This tale belongs to Type 953 in the Aarne-Thompson classification. S. Ó Súilleabháin and R. Christiansen, in *The Types of the Irish Folktale*, give full information about manuscript sources of other Irish oral versions of the tale and printed sources of versions recorded in Ireland. The tale is 191a in Grimm's *Deutsche Hausmärchen* (see Bolte-Polivka, III, 369). It is a frame-story and is discussed by Stith Thompson in *The Folktale* ([New York, 1946], p. 172). A version close to this one, recorded in the neighboring island of Inishmaan, was published without translation in *Béaloideas*, 4 (1934), 182–189. Summarized forms of the story are given by J. Curtin, *Hero-Tales of Ireland* ([London, 1894], pp. 93–113), by Joseph Jacobs, *Celtic Fairy Tales* ([London, 1892], pp. 34–46), and by Thackeray in his *Irish Sketch Book* (ch. 16).

Readers will notice the recurrent formulae, sometimes called *runs*, which correspond to the formulae in the Homeric poems and are a characteristic feature of oral narrative. A. B. Lord in *The Singer of Tales* ([Cambridge, Mass., 1960], pp. 30–67) and G. S. Kirk in *The Songs of Homer* ([Cambridge, Eng., 1962], pp. 59–68) have discussed the matter. Another notable feature is the introduction of motifs that have no apparent relevance and seem designed merely to promote a sense of wonder: for example, the chair breaking when the king's son under *geasa* sits on it, or the two infants in the Black Thief's house.

The word *geasa* has been left untranslated because there is no exact equivalent for it. The context makes clear that *geasa* are magical prohibitions or commands which are placed by one person upon another and which entail severe penalties if violated. The motif of the *geis* frequently occurs in medieval Irish sagas (see J. R. Reinhard, *The Survival of Geis in Medieval Romance* [Halle, 1933]). *Yeenach raw* is a mere phonetic rendering of corrupt words probably no longer understood by the storyteller.

The Queen of the Island of Loneliness

The story belongs to Type 551. Full information about manuscript and printed sources of other Irish oral versions is contained in Ó Súilleabháin and Christiansen. References to the tale as found in other countries are given in Aarne-Thompson, *The Types of the Folktale* (p. 197). The tale is 97 in Grimm's *Deutsche Hausmärchen* (Bolte-Polivka, II, 394).

The motif of identification by matching parts of a divided token (H100) is not followed up; the narrator evidently forgot to bring the torn napkin back into the story at the proper moment. The swelling of the hero's hands in the gloves when he is in danger is a motif like D1317, Magic Object Warns of Danger. The suit that squeezes until the wearer tells the truth is like D1316.8, Magic Collar Indicates Falsehood by Squeezing Throat.

Foreword

The Giant of the Mighty Blows

This is a version of The Dragon-Slayer, Type 300, which forms one of the episodes in the legend of Perseus (as rescuer of Andromeda) and is called the "Herdsman Type" by Hartland (*The Legend of Perseus*, III [London, 1896], 3), who refers to two Irish versions, one by J. Curtin, *Myths and Folk-Lore of Ireland* ([Boston, 1906], pp. 157-174). and another by W. Larminie, *West Irish Folk-Tales and Romances* ([London, 1893], pp. 196-210). The story is very common in Ireland, and Christiansen chose it as a type for discussion in his article "Towards a Printed List of Irish Fairy-Tales," *Béaloideas*, 7 (1937), 3-14. He gives a good analysis of Irish versions (p. 8), of which thirty-six are mentioned as published. There are more than four hundred in the archives of the Irish Folklore Commission, according to Ó Súilleabháin and Christiansen (pp. 58-62).

The transcript breaks off owing to failure of the dictaphone at the point where the giants' mother appears. From this point on, the translation is from a version in *Béaloideas,* 8 (1938), 201-211, recorded in west Mayo and entitled "An Deachmhaidh" ("The Tithe"), as is Larminie's story. The Irish text of this part begins in *Béaloideas,* 8, at page 207 and is here translated with the kind permission of the director of the Irish Folklore Commission.

A different story with the title "Fathach Mór na mBuillí" ("The Giant of the Mighty Blows") was recorded from the same narrator, Joe Flaherty, by Ciarán Bairéad in 1958 and is in the archives of the Commission, volume 1488, page 197.

We may thus find the same story under various titles, and different stories under the same title, in the oral tradition that has survived.

The Knowledge of the Only Story and the Dúdán's Sword

As this is not an international folktale, it has no place in Aarne-Thompson's classification and does not appear in Ó Súilleabháin and Christiansen either. But although the story is Irish, there are motifs that are common in folklore: the imposing of a task as the result of losing a game and the transformation of a man into various animal forms (which occurs in the medieval Welsh tale "Math Son of Mathonwy").

In this version the story is more heavily loaded with formulae than the other stories told by Joe Flaherty. The formulae are familiar, known by heart to the listeners, and are for them a welcome ornament. In one place (p. 90) a formula is used where it is quite unsuitable, which shows the extent to which these runs are mere aids to the storyteller. A similar use, or misuse, of runs has recently been observed by a Romanian folklorist, but the exact reference is not readily available; for analogous use of epic formulae, see Milman Parry, *L'Épithète traditionelle dans Homère* (Paris, 1928), pp. 146–181, and *Studies in the Epic Technique of Oral Verse-Making*, Harvard Studies in Classical Philology, 41 (1930), 137–147.

This tale provides good illustrations of the very simple style proper to the folktale. Subordination is avoided, so that there are very few relative or dependent clauses: " 'Oh!' said he, 'that is a magician and he could kill the whole world.' " "He slept well that night, and very well, and in the morning

Foreword

he got up, and, by dad, the farmer was up before him! He had breakfast ready, a good breakfast, and he ate it. Then he gave him a horse."

The story is an exact translation of the narrative. Words not heard or otherwise doubtful are in parentheses. In a few places where the speaker said "he," the Wizard, the King of Ireland's Son, the farmer, or the Goblin (who is commonly referred to as "the farmer") is specified in translation. It is not without interest that where "he" in the spoken narrative is quite sufficient, the written form seems to require more exact reference.

Terror without Fear

This opens with motif H942, Tasks Assigned as Payment of Gambling Loss, which is well known in Irish stories. After the hero acquires a wife and a helper, the wife is abducted by the three Sharachauns, who belong to Type 1950, The Three Lazy Ones. They have taken her to the land of Fionn Mhac Cumhaill, the leader of the Fianna in the Fenian cycle, which flourished in the late Middle Irish period and survives in oral tradition. Goll Mhac Morna is the leader of a rival faction and Oscar is Fionn's grandson and the son of Oisín (not mentioned here). Fionn's Thumb of Knowledge (D1811.1.1) is a commonplace of the cycle (see R. D. Scott, *The Thumb of Knowledge* [New York, 1930]). A voyage over the sea such as that made by Terror without Fear in search of his wife is a common feature of Irish tales. The rusting of a knife to indicate the death of someone absent is E761.4 in Thompson's *Motif-Index*. The motif of Fionn's disguising himself as a child in a cradle (K1839.12) is paralleled by a story published in *Béaloideas*, 2 (1930), 221–222, 226–227. "Terror without Fear" contains some fine runs, which are not identical in every occurrence. The teller's style may have been affected by interruptions made by the writer in keeping pace with him.

Both *Mac* and *Mhac* occur in proper names, as Inisheer is a border area between north and south. In northern dialects *Mac* is usually lenited in apposition and is pronounced [wak].

MYLES DILLON
Dublin, Ireland

there was a king in ireland

the black thief

THERE WAS A TIME LONG AGO, it's long ago it was. If I'd been there then, I wouldn't be here now. I'd have a new story or an old story or I'd be a gray-haired old storyteller. For there was a king in Ireland long ago, and he was married and had a young son. It was well and it wasn't ill. God sent for the young queen and she died. The king used to be hunting and harrying every day for himself, and the boy was growing up. Some of his counselors came to him and said that he was spending his life badly by not marrying again. "But even so—," he said, "I don't want to give my son a stepmother, and if it were not for that—"

"There is no good in that," said they. "You will have to do it."

He went and got himself a young queen, and he married, and it was well and it wasn't ill; after a year and a day a son was born to him, and after another year and a day another son was born to him. The eldest son that he had by his first wife was growing up till he was grown and strong; and then he was going out hunting and harrying along with him, the eldest boy — and when he was, there's not a wild beast in the forest nor a deer nor anything he would meet, but he was the first to bring it down with his gun.

That was well until the other two grew up, and then all three used to go along with him, hunting and harrying. Every day that was their employment, and, by dad, one day the young queen said —. He was very fond of the eldest boy, he was much fonder of him than he was of the other two. She didn't know in the world what to do, and so it was that she went one day and pretended that she was sick. She took to her bed, and she killed a young cock and put its blood into a bottle, and then she lay very sick in her bed.

When the king came in, "Where is the young lady?" said he to the maid.

"Oh, by this and by that, she is very sick in bed!" said she.

He went to her room. "How are you?" said he.

She turned around and put a mouthful of the blood into her mouth and then spat it out onto his chest.

"Oh, you're very sick!" said he. "That is your heart's blood that you are spitting."

"I am sick indeed," said she, "and perhaps you would leave your eldest son with me for company."

"Is that what you'd like?" said he. "Very well," said he.

Next morning he told the eldest boy to stay with her for company that day, and he and the two others went off hunting and harrying. They went off out into the forest, and when she saw that they were gone, she got up, and she and the King of Ireland's eldest son were together. She got a table and a pack of cards. "King of Ireland's Son," said she, "would you play a game of cards?"

"By dad," said he, "I never missed a pastime."

They began to play, and they played for a while, and, by dad, the King of Ireland's Son won the game. And when the King of Ireland's Son won the game, they went on playing

The Black Thief

and the queen won the next game. "Both of us are satisfied now," said the King of Ireland's Son.

"Oh!" said she, "you'll know soon enough! I place you under *geasa* of heavy magic not to sleep two nights on the same bed nor to eat two meals at the same table until you go to the western world and fetch me three brown horses that Seán Mac Veenglish has. You tell your *geasa* now!" said she to the King of Ireland's Son.

"Well, you'll know soon enough!" said he. "I place you under *geasa* of heavy magic not to sleep two nights on the same bed nor to eat two meals at the same table, but to go out now before me and stand over there on the east gable of the church with a cambric needle in the middle and a sheaf of oats on the west gable, and to eat or drink nothing but what comes to you from the sheaf of oats through the needle's eye."

"God save us!" said she. "Free me and I will free you!"

"Stand by the *geasa* you have laid on me!" said he.

Next morning she had to go out before him and stand on the east gable of the church with the cambric needle in the middle and the sheaf of oats on the west gable.

By dad, it was well and it wasn't ill. The two other brothers said, "Wherever you go, we'll go along with you."

He set out, and the two others went along with him, and they were traveling and traveling until the bright light of the day was going from them, the darkness of the night was coming toward them, the white nag going behind the dock-leaf, and *yeenach raw* from the dock-leaf, if she waited at all for it. They didn't see sight of deer or damsel. "By dad, we'll be out all night," said the King of Ireland's Son.

"We will indeed," said the other two.

They came to the edge of a forest, and when they reached it, the King of Ireland's Son said, "The best thing for us to do now is to go into the wood and climb into a tree, and that is how we'll be safest." For night had fallen. They went in and climbed into a tree and settled there till morning. But in the still of the night wild beasts came out, when they smelt them up in the trees, and went rushing against the tree, and bending and twisting it, but they could not bring it down. When morning came, the wild beasts went into the forest, and they came down onto the road and went on their way till they were far, far from home. They saw a little light in the distance, and it was far away. They made for it with haste and hurry, and it was dark night when they reached the house. They knocked at the door, and it was opened, and in they went. The man that opened it was a middle-aged farmer.

"God save you!" said they.

"God save you kindly," said the farmer. "You are welcome," said he. "You must be strangers, for I do not know you." He gave them chairs, and when the King of Ireland's Son sat down, the chair broke under him. "Oh!" said he, "you are a king's son under *geasa*. Would it be any harm to ask what *geasa* have been laid on you?"

"No harm at all," said the King of Ireland's Son. And he began to tell his story.

"Oh!" said he, "I spent seven years trying to steal one of those horses and I failed. I am the man they call the Black Thief, and I will go along with you tomorrow. Maybe we'll succeed, and maybe we won't."

He gave them supper, plenty of oatmeal stirabout and goat's milk, and they ate it. There were two big cradles beside the hearth and a child in each cradle. When they had finished their supper, they were watching the man. He got supper for the children, and then he cleaned their faces—they were a girl and a boy—he cleaned the girl with his tongue, her mouth, her nose, and every bit of her, and he wiped the boy's face with his bib, and then he laid them down.

When he had finished, the King of Ireland's Son said, "Would it be any harm to ask why you did that to the children, to clean one of them with his bib—his mouth and all—and the other with your tongue?"

"No harm at all," said he. "That is my mother and this is my father, and they are in second childhood. That is the way they reared me, and I am giving them the same care in the very same way. My mother used to wipe my mouth and my nose with her tongue, and my father used to wipe my mouth and my nose in my bib, and I am doing the same with them."

"I see," said the King of Ireland's Son.

By dad, so it was. They got a bed to go to sleep, and then he said, "Don't hurry at all to get up in the morning until I call you and your breakfast is ready." Next morning, as soon as ever the sun rose, the King of Ireland's Son got up, and your man was up before him! And when he was, he had his breakfast ready, plenty more oatmeal stirabout and plenty of goat's milk. And when they had eaten it, he said, "Now I'll go out to a little house where there is an old woman, and I'll call on her to look after those two until I come back, if I do come back. But sure, if I don't, it can't be helped." By dad, out he went, and when he had brought her in, he left her there to look after the children. He went along with them then, and there were four of them, three of themselves and the Black Thief.

They were traveling then and traveling, until the bright light of the day was going from them, the darkness of night coming toward them, the white nag going behind the dock-leaf, and *yeenach raw* from the dock-leaf, if she waited at all for it, until it was high evening of the day.

"Now," said the Thief, "we'll make a halt here. I know where the house is. And four girls will come with bales of hay from a certain haycock, and we will get into them and hide there." They took his advice, and just then the girls came, and each of them filled an enormous bale of hay, the full load of each one, and they never stopped until they came to the very spot where the men were; and there they rested and laid down the bales. When they had laid down the bales, one of them began to sing a tune, and the other three began to dance to the lively music. "Now, you rascals," said the Black Thief, "let each of us try to crawl in under a bale. If they begin bringing the hay to throw it to the horses, we need try no better way of getting into the stable that the horses are in, but to go in under a bale of hay."

By dad, they tried it. They went into the hay as best they could, and when the girls had stopped — they were well tired dancing — one of them took the bale of hay on her back. "Good Lord!" said she. "This bale is so heavy that I shan't be able to carry it."

"Ah, it's not," said one of the others, "but you're tired from

The Black Thief

the dancing." Another took it on her back, and when that other took it on her back, she said the same, until each one of them took a bale on her back, and they all said there was no telling the terrible weight that was in those bales. They went off and never stopped or stayed till they went into the stable where Seán Mac Veenglish kept the horses.

They gave the hay to the horses, and when they did, the stable was locked, and the horses were eating the hay until the dead of night. Then the Black Thief said to the youngest son of the King of Ireland, "Get up and see could you get a hold of the brown horse." He got up, and he was going to and fro until after a while he got a hold of her, but she gave a loud neigh that was heard throughout the seven kingdoms. Seán Mac Veenglish was in bed, and he was thrown against the ceiling, and he fell down so that one of his ribs was broken. Oh! he rang the bell then for them to be up lively and very lively and out to the horses, that the Black Thief was outside trying to steal the horses!

By dad, it was well and it wasn't ill. The lads made no delay till they were out, and they searched the stable high and low and found nothing. They came in and said there was nobody there, and that he must have been dreaming.

The house settled down, and when it did and it was later in the night, the Black Thief said, "Get up quickly, second son of the King of Ireland, and see if you can get a hold of the black horse!" He got up and tried to get a hold of her, and when he tried, she gave a neigh and a cry that was heard throughout the seven kingdoms; and Seán Mac Veenglish was thrown up against the ceiling and down again so that another rib was broken. Then he rang the bell and called on the boys to be out quickly and very quickly, because the Black Thief was in the horses' stable.

Out they went, and made no delay, till they searched the stable high and low, and they found nothing. They came in. "Oh!" they said, "it is dreaming you were. There is nobody there."

By dad, he settled down again, and when he did, later in the night, the Black Thief said, "Eldest son of the King of Ireland, you rascal, get up quickly and see could you get a hold of the white horse!" He jumped up and made no delay and tried to get a hold of her, and she gave a neigh and a cry and shook herself, and he got no good of her.

Seán Mac Veenglish was thrown up against the ceiling and down again, and another rib was broken. He rang the bell again. "Out with you quick and very quick! The Black Thief is stealing the horses! Have you searched under the horses' heads? Have you searched in the hay?"

"No," said the boys.

"Well, search the hay now," said he, "and maybe you will find him."

They went out and searched, and, by dad, they were all found and taken; and they brought the four of them in. "Oh!" said he to the Black Thief, "you're caught at last!"

"I am indeed," said the Black Thief. "It can't be helped." They were raised up and hung from the top of the house with a wisp of tow burning under their noses.

There they were, with a wisp of tow burning under their

The Black Thief

noses. "Now," said he to the Black Thief, "were you ever in a worse plight than you are now?"

"Indeed I was," said the Black Thief, "and a hundred and a thousand times worse."

"Would you tell the story," said he.

"I would if you would let me down, with the eldest son of the King of Ireland."

"Why wouldn't I?" said Seán Mac Veenglish. Then the Black Thief began his story.

"Well," he said, "I was on patrol, as often I was, and I was going to a fair with a bull and two cows, and I was going in the dead of the night past a graveyard, when a cat came out toward me and then another cat, saying, 'Food, food or conflict, or your own bones to pick!' That is what the cats said to me. 'There is one of the beasts for you,' said I. I gave them one of the beasts. And when I did, I went off driving the other cow and the bull before me, giving them the stick till I had gone a fair distance.

"It wasn't long till a cat caught up with me, and another and another and another. 'Food, food or conflict,' they said, 'or your own bones to pick!' I looked at them, and if there was one cat there, there were a thousand cats there. 'There is another of the beasts for you,' said I. They set upon her, and indeed it did not take them long to devour her, and she was bellowing. I drove off with my bull. The bull was all I had left, and I drove him off.

"I was driving him along as fast as I could, giving him the stick, and while I was on my way, it wasn't long till the cat came up with me again. 'Food, food or conflict,' said she, 'or your own bones to pick!' I looked at her, and when I looked, if there was one cat there, there was a shoal of cats. 'Oh! here he is for you,' said I. I gave them the bull. They went for my poor bull, and he began to bellow so that you would hear him a mile from home. And there wasn't a hair on his hide but that a cat had a hold on it.

"I was on my way then as fast as I was able to travel, and I hadn't gone far at all when the cats came up with me again. 'Food, food or conflict,' they said, 'or your own bones to pick!' By dad, I put my finger into my mouth and gave a long, low, sweet whistle calling on my dogs of hunting and hounding to come right quickly, for I had the grandest hunting in Ireland for them. Oh! a cat ran east and a cat ran west, a cat ran up and a cat ran down. In a quarter of an hour there wasn't a single cat to be seen.

"Isn't that a worse plight," said he, "than for someone to put a wisp of tow under my nose?"

"By dad, it was a great plight," said he, "but you'll have to go up again." Up with him again and there was a wisp of tow burning under the poor fellow's nose, and when there was, "You are caught anyhow," (said Seán Mac Veenglish). "Now were you ever in a worse plight than this?" said he.

"Indeed I was," said the Black Thief, "and a hundred and a thousand times greater."

"Would you tell the story?" said he.

"I would," he said, "if you let me down, with the second son of the King of Ireland." They were let down.

"Well," he said, "I was traveling one day far, far from

The Black Thief

home, and it was snowing, and snowing heavily, and I had a little dog, and all I could do was to keep on going. I was lost and I didn't know where I was going. When it got late, night overtook me, and when night overtook me, I saw smoke coming up through the snow. I made for the smoke, and, by dad, I could not find a door nor any way to get in, so I went up onto the roof and listened through the chimney. What did I hear but three giant hags who had made a Sword of Light, and what were they saying but that the Black Thief was going to steal it from them next morning, and that they did not know where to hide the sword! 'I'll put it under my pillow,' said one of them, 'and the Thief will have no chance of stealing it.'

"I was listening, and I lay down in the snow. I had nowhere to go in the house until the hags went asleep. And when I thought they must be asleep, I went down the chimney and opened the door, and when I did, I heard the hags snoring so that they drew in the two sides of the house with every snore they made. They were fast asleep. I was stealing over to where the sword was, and I reached it and took it away with me. Out I went then onto the street, and I said to myself, wherever I went, that they would find my footsteps in the snow. I went up on the side-wall of the house, and lay down in the snow, and it was snowing so hard that I was covered by the snow up on the side-wall of the house. There I lay with the Sword of Light.

"In the morning, when the hags got up, the sword was gone. That is when the three of them fell upon each other so that they were fighting and killing each other, and they didn't know which of them would get satisfaction from the other for the sword being stolen. Out they went on to the street to see whether they could find my footsteps anywhere, and they couldn't. But as they turned back, one of them chanced to look up, and the snow was melting away from me as I lay on the side of the house. She saw me up on the side-wall of the house, lying in the snow. They cried out then that they had caught the Thief, that he was up on the side-wall of the house! That was when each one of them set to work, one at each wing of the house, and myself above! By dad, I put my finger in my mouth and gave a long, low, sweet whistle, calling my dogs of hunting and hounding to come right quickly, for I had then the finest hunting in Ireland, if they would like to hunt hags. Oh! one hag went east and another went west, and in a quarter of an hour there was no trace of them. And I went off with the sword I had stolen from the hags.

"Was that not a worse plight than for you to be burning a wisp of tow under my nose?"

"By dad, it was bad enough," said Seán Mac Veenglish, "but even so, you will have to go up again." He was hung up again, with wisp of tow burning under his nose. "Now," said Seán Mac Veenglish, "were you ever in a worse plight than you are in at present?"

"Indeed, I was," said the Black Thief, "a hundred and a thousand times worse."

"Would you tell the story?"

"I would," said he, "if you will let me down, with the youngest son of the King of Ireland."

The Black Thief

"Why wouldn't I let you down, if you'll tell the story?"

"I will tell it," said the Black Thief. He let them down, and when he did—

"Well," said he, "I was one day, as often I was, going on patrol, and I was in the forest and my little dog there with me. I saw smoke a good distance off in the forest, and I made toward it and came to a house. In the house there was a fine young woman, to give her her due, and I greeted her and she greeted me kindly, and I asked her could she give me food, saying that I was hungry and thirsty, and she said she could. It was well and it wasn't ill, she got me a meal and I ate it, a splendid meal. I sat down then, and she had a fine little child, to give it its due, in her arms. She had a knife in her hand, and she made as though to stab the child, but as she was about it, the child laughed. Again she tried to stab the child, and again the child laughed.

" 'Oh!' said I, 'why are you going to kill the child?'

" 'I must kill him,' said she, 'I am married to a giant, and he is gone to the western world, hunting and harrying, and I must have the heart and liver of the child and the big toe of his right foot cooked for him when he comes home.'

" 'Is that the way?' said I.

" 'It is,' said she.

" 'It is a great pity to kill the child,' said I. 'You'll see what we'll do. I will kill the little dog, and take out the heart and liver, and do you cut the big toe of his right foot off the child, and that will not harm him greatly. The giant will not know that the heart and liver are of the dog and not of the child.

You can cook the heart and liver of the dog, and the big toe of the child's right foot, and you can hide the child where he won't find it.'

" 'By dad, you are right!' said she.

"I killed the dog, and she cut off the big toe of the child's right foot; and away she went and hid the child somewhere outside.

"They were put down to boil then, the heart and the liver and the big toe. 'Now,' said she, 'you had better be off, for if you don't go, he will kill you. He has a room up there full of corpses. There are hundreds of them there thrown on top of each other.'

" 'I wouldn't have got away before he would come,' said I. 'There is no good in my going. I had better stay where I am.'

" 'He will have you for supper surely,' said she.

"With that I heard the storm approaching from the western world, the bottom of the forest being driven to the top and the top to the bottom, the old tree trembling and the young tree bending, as he came with a great beast on the end of his stick and a dead hag on his shoulder. It was well and it wasn't ill. He came to the outside and threw down the hag. I ran back and hid among the corpses.

" 'Foo, faw, feet-yogue,' said he, 'I smell an Irishman hidden in sooth!'

" 'I saw no one about,' said she, 'except a beggar, a stranger from Ireland out there. What is the use in your searching for him?'

" 'Is that the way?' said he, and in he came, and he was very hungry. 'Have you got that ready?' said he.

" 'I have,' said she.

" 'That's good,' said he. He ate it up, and then he stood up. 'I have nothing in that much,' said he. He went into the room, and he brought a sword and a knife, and began cutting up the corpses. He cut a slice off me from my ear down to my rump from where I lay among the corpses. I did not make a sound. Out he came and he ate that piece. 'There is grand fresh meat in there,' he said. 'If I had a short sleep, I would have a fine meal.' He went in and fetched out a pile of goatskins and stretched himself out fast asleep on the floor. He was snoring enough to draw in the two sides of the house. Then I got up, when I heard him snoring, and looked around —though I was pouring blood—and what did I see leaning against the wall but a big grape-fork that he had, for lifting fish out of the river when he was down catching them. And I said to myself, if I had it red hot, that it was just the measure of his eyes, of the giant's eyes. I crept over to the fire and put in the fork and reddened it, and came over to the giant, while I had the chance, and stuck the fork into his eyes.

"By dad, the giant jumped up. 'You ruffianly schemer!' said he to his wife, 'I said that I got the smell of an Irishman. Go out now and drive in the fat sheep that are there outside so that I may eat my fill before I die!' She went out and drove them in, twenty or thirty of them; and as soon as some of them were in, I caught one and began to flay it as fast as I could. And your man was at the door. When all the sheep were in, he said, 'Now drive them out here, and they will go out between my legs, and I will keep the fattest one I find.' He began to feel them, as they went out between his legs as he stood in the doorway. They were going out one by one, and any one that he pinched and that was fat, he would tell his wife to drive it back into the room and keep it. He was keeping back an odd one as they poured out; and I was flaying away as hard as I could, until I had one flayed, and the skin ready. I put the skin on my back and over my head, and went out between the giant's legs, with the skin on my back. The giant felt my back. 'Oh!' said he, 'here is a fine fat sheep!' But I was nearly out, and I jumped up and out, and left the skin in his hands.

" 'Oh!' said he, 'you have escaped!'

" 'I have,' said I.

" 'Well,' said he, 'there is a ring for you that you will have always, and any day that you call on me for help or counsel, I shall be there. There is the ring for you, and put it on your finger.'

"By dad, he threw the ring to me. 'Have you got it?' said he.

" 'I have,' said I.

" ' It is on your finger?' said he.

" 'Yes,' said I.

" 'Squeeze, ring, squeeze!' said he. 'Where are you now?'

" 'Oh! I am here,' said the ring. The giant leaped out and thought to catch a hold of me, but I jumped to one side.

"It was well, and leave it so. 'Where are you now ring?' he kept calling.

"And the ring would answer, 'I'm here.' It was on my finger. The giant would leap forward and try to catch me, but he couldn't see for his eye was gone. And so it went on till I was tired out. Each time he came up with me I used to jump to one side, until we came to a great wide river, and the giant was after me all the time. I chanced to find a stone and I struck my finger with the stone and struck off my finger and threw it far out into the river.

" 'Where are you now, ring?' said the giant.

" 'I'm here,' said the ring. The giant gave a great leap out into the river.

"It was well and it wasn't ill. He was going out into the current as fast as he could. I seized a great stone, as heavy as I could lift, and hurled it down on his head and killed him. 'Now you have your deserts!' said I.

"Was that not as great a plight as for you to burn a wisp of tow under my nose," said he, "and was it not a greater action?"

"By dad, it was great action," said Seán Mac Veenglish.

"And it is the very truth that he is telling you," said his wife. "And to prove it," said she, "you have lost the big toe of your right foot. You were the child whom the woman had that day and that she was going to kill. If it had not been for this man with his little dog, you would have been killed. You were saved just as he has told you. And to prove it, take off your shoes, and the big toe of your right foot is gone."

By dad, he took off his shoe, and the big toe of his right foot was gone from Seán Mac Veenglish!

Then indeed they didn't know how they could do enough for him. They gave him his dinner, and to each one of them, and they did not know how to do enough honor to the Thief and the three sons of the King of Ireland. They stayed several days and got splendid food and everything of the best; and when they were leaving for home, each of them got a horse.

Each man of them got one of the brown horses. The three sons of the King of Ireland got one each, and the Black Thief got one for himself in reward for what he did and all he had suffered.

Away with them then, and they never stopped or stayed until they came to the Thief's house. When they reached the house, the old woman was there looking after the children, and they spent the night with the Thief, a third of it with Fenian tales and a third of it with stories. And indeed it is many a tight place that the Black Thief had been in. Then they said farewell to the Thief and came home to the King of Ireland; and the woman they had left on the church roof was frozen to an icicle. And the King made over to his eldest son the house and all it contained, and he made him heir to the kingdom.

the queen of the island of loneliness

There was a time long ago, it's long ago it was. If I'd been there then I wouldn't be here now. I would have a new story or an old story or I'd be a gray-haired old storyteller. For there was a king in Ireland long ago, and he had two sons, and one day he was hunting and harrying out into the forest, and as he turned back home—he had three islands three miles out to sea—and with his field glasses he saw smoke rising from one of the islands. By dad, when he did, he came home in sorrow and told his wife that he saw smoke rising from one of the islands.

"Oh," said she, "by this and by that, are you and your two sons not crew enough, and go out," said she, "to the island and find out what is there."

"Oh," said he, "it is a great giant who has come from the Eastern World or the Western World and settled there, and it is little good for me to go there, for it is hard to kill that giant or to drive him away."

"How do you know?" said she. "Go as far as him, and you will know what is there."

The next morning, as early as the sun rose he rose. He got ready a ship and set out. He found a crew and his two sons, and he never stopped or stayed till he landed at the quay at the end of the island. He berthed his ship at the quay and settled her for a year and a day, so that she could see the Fianna of Ireland and the women of the world, and neither man nor woman could see her.

He walked on up, and never stopped or stayed till he saw a house in the distance, and he made his way toward it. When he came to it, he went in, and there he found a charming lady. By dad, when he did, he spoke to her and they greeted each other, and she gave him supper, and he sat down and ate his fill.

"Is there any one coming to this house but you?" said he.

"There is not," said she.

By dad, they stayed like that until night, and she got ready his bed and he went to sleep, and she made another bed for herself on the other side.

"Now," said he, "if there's no one coming into the house but the two of us, wouldn't one bed be enough for us?"

"By dad, it would," said she.

He went in with the young woman, and when he did—the next morning she put a sleeping-pin into him, and there you may leave him for three times three months.

When three times three months was over, by dad, she took out the sleeping-pin. "Get up now," said she, "and baptize your son." She had a baby son!

"Oh my God!" said he, 'if I am as long here as that you have a son by me, I have neither house nor home, I haven't a cock of hay, I haven't a ship either that isn't swept away, if I am that long here!"

"Oh, everything is safe," said she. "Your men are safe, for

The Queen of the Island of Loneliness

I sent plenty of provisions to them to the ship, and everything is safe. Get up now," said she, "and baptize your son!"

"I baptize him," said he, "the son of the King of Ireland and the Queen of the Island of Loneliness." It was well and it wasn't ill then. He set out and never stopped or stayed till he came to the ship and the crew were all right in the ship, and he sailed away.

He never stopped or stayed until he reached home, and, by dad, when he reached home, everything was safe. He stayed like that for fifteen years, and then, by dad, the King of Norway made war against the King of Ireland.

The boy was growing up till he was over fifteen years of age by this time, and when he was, he used to be hunting and harrying out in the forest with his gun. He came in one day, and when he came in that day, his mother said, "Oh, son, have you any news?"

"No," said he. "Where would I get news? From the birds of the air or the wild beasts of the forest?"

"Well," said his mother, "I am not so, for I have news."

"Where would you get it?" said he.

"Oh, I have it," said she. "The King of Ireland is at war. The King of Norway has made war on him, and you should go and help him."

"How would I know even who he is?" said the boy.

"I'll give you a napkin," said she, "and all you have to do is to show the half-napkin, for the King of Ireland has the other half, and the two halves will fit together, and then," said she, "you will know who you are."

"Very well," said he.

Next morning as early as the sun rose he rose, and when he got up, he got ready his ship and sailed away. He never stopped or stayed till he came to land down in the harbor.

"Well," said she, "the first regiment you meet, go down the second road, and if they are the regiment of the King of Ireland, they will greet you kindly, and let them pass. But if they are the regiment of the King of Norway, they will give you not a greeting but a curse; and attack them and kill them, and do the same with the next regiment."

It was well and it wasn't ill, he came to land and made his way up, sword in hand, and he greeted the first regiment he met, and they gave him not a greeting but a curse. He attacked them with his sword, and he began killing over him and under him till he had slaughtered them all.

The next regiment he saw, he approached them and greeted them in the same way, and they gave him not a greeting but a curse. He attacked them in the same way, and he never stopped or stayed at them, from once he began to kill them until he had killed them all. He went on then and met the third regiment, and when he met the third regiment he greeted them, and they greeted him with a welcome, and, by dad, he did not interfere with them. The battle was over, and the King of Ireland had won the day.

It was well and it wasn't ill then. He went in to the King of Ireland, and nobody knew where in the world the warrior had come from. [Here the storyteller has apparently omitted the episode of the napkin of recognition.] He spent a week or a fortnight there, and when he had spent a full fortnight, he sailed away again and came home, after saying farewell to the King of Ireland.

He was at home then for half a year, and, by dad, the King of Norway heard again that a certain warrior had been killed, and he made war again on the King of Ireland—after half a year, that was all the respite he gave him.

One day there, when he came in from hunting, his mother was waiting for him. "God save you, son!" said she.

"God and Mary save you!" said the King of Ireland's Son.

"Have you any news?" said she.

"No," said he. "Where would I get it? From the birds of the air or the wild beasts of the forest?"

"Oh, I am not so," said she.

"How is that?" said he.

"Oh," said she, "the King of Norway is making war on the King of Ireland, and unless you go to him, there won't be a head left on a body. You must go to him tomorrow. Tomorrow you must go to the King of Ireland, for there is war and bloodshed."

"I will not go," said he. "How would I know even who he is?"

"Go, son!" said she, "for the King of Norway will kill him and all his people; and you will have only two blows to strike, and I will go along with you. Here is a pair of gloves for you, and whenever an enemy is coming against you, your hands will begin to swell in the gloves, and you will know that an enemy is approaching."

He set out and sailed away the next morning. He never stopped or stayed till he came to the land of the King of Ireland, and when he did, he went up to them—the King of Norway had drawn up his regiments. And the first regiment he met, he greeted them, and they gave him not a greeting but a curse. He attacked them with his sword and began to kill them under him and over him till he had killed the whole regiment. With the next regiment he did the same, and then he greeted the third regiment, and when he did, by dad, they greeted him in return.

It was well and it wasn't ill. The King of Ireland took him home with him and gave him a great welcome. By dad, he kept him there for a few months, and when he was a few months there, the King of Ireland's wife pretended to be sick, and she was very sick entirely, and nothing would cure her. The King of Ireland asked what was wrong with her, or was there anything in the world that would cure her. She said that nothing in the world would cure her, unless she got three bottles of water from Teentagh's Well.

"Oh," said the king, "that is a big job!"

By dad, the boy was listening to him. "We will go," said he. "Your two sons and I will go to fetch it, wherever it is to be found."

It was well and it wasn't ill. Next morning they got ready a ship and dressed themselves up, and their crew, and sailed away and turned toward the west. They traveled and traveled till it was late evening, and there was no sign of land or shore or anything else. So they remained. They made the ship fast, and the King of Ireland's eldest son took the watch, and the boy, the son of the King of Ireland and the Queen of the Island of Loneliness, went to sleep. He and the young son went to

The Queen of the Island of Loneliness

sleep, and the other stayed on watch on the ship until daybreak; and she had traveled a good distance during the night, and they sailed on for a good while into the day.

"Go aloft," said he to the young fellow, "and bring your telescope and try whether you can see sign of deer or damsel far or near, or any sort of land!" He went, and he saw nothing.

They were sailing on, and while they were, he said to the second man to go aloft; and he went, and he said that he saw land in the distance, but that it was far away. They made for it as best they could, and late in the evening at last they came in under the shore of a fine fertile island with a fine sandy beach.

By dad, they went ashore out of the ship and laid her up on the beach, and when they did, he gave her a kick in the stern that sent her seven hundred yards up onto the grass. And he put a handful of fine-blown sand over her, so that the Fianna of Ireland would not see her nor the women of the world, and that she could see both man and woman.

He went off then, and they all walked up, and they saw a fine courtly house, and they made for it and came right into it. They were made welcome, being strangers, and got a good meal, and they were discussing the world and the weather, when the men of the house asked them where they were going or what brought them that way.

The son of the King of Ireland and the Queen of the Island of Loneliness told him that it was in search of three bottles of water from the Well of Teentagh that they came that way.

"Oh, God help you!" said he. "Sure, you can't get that!

That water is so well guarded that no one can get it. There is a great courtly house with three fences around it and a gate in each fence. There are two poisonous boars outside before the first gate, one at each side, and two poisonous hounds inside at the middle gate, one at each side, and two poisonous dogs at the innermost gate, and nothing can get in by that gate. Save only this," said he, "that they spend half the year asleep and half the year awake, and maybe you would have the luck to find them asleep."

By dad, life went out of the two boys and not a drop remained in their veins at the story that the man told them, but the King of Ireland's Son was without trouble or fear.

"Now," said the man, "tomorrow I will give you a gray horse that will jump the gate, and maybe they are asleep. If they are, you are all right. Ask no questions if they are asleep. Go in, and the horse will jump every gate until you reach the great courtyard. The well is down at the end of the courtyard. Fill your three bottles there, for that is the water of the Well of Teentagh."

Next morning, he gave him the horse, and, by dad, he made for the gate, and in went the horse. He had a sword in each hand, and sure enough the two boars were asleep. There wasn't one of them that wasn't snoring. He paid no heed to them, but on he went and jumped the next gate, and the two hounds were asleep, one at each side. He went on over the next gate, and the two dogs were asleep, and he stood watching them and asked no questions. He halted his horse and rode no further, but came down off him. And when he did so, he never stopped or stayed, and he traveled through the court-

The Queen of the Island of Loneliness

yard till he came to the well. He found the bottles and filled the three bottles with water from the Well of Teentagh.

He was making his way out, and in no hurry at all, and he saw a door to one side all covered with gold, and it was half open. By dad, when it was, he pushed in the door, and looked in to see what was inside in the room. By dad, he saw a fine bed, and a grand lady in the bed! "Indeed," said he, "wouldn't I be a miserable man not to go in beside you!" It was well and it wasn't ill. In he went to bed beside the young lady, and there he stayed. After he had done his part, he went off and brought his bottles along with him. He came to the court where he had left his two companions dead, when life had left them with fright, and he rubbed a drop of the water on them, the water of the Well of Teentagh, and they rose up as hale and hearty as ever they were, and they all went off together. They never stayed, not forever, until they reached the ship.

Then they reached the ship, and when they did, they sailed away and traveled east until they came to the coast of Ireland.

When they had landed, he put on the gloves, and, by dad, his hands began to swell in the gloves, and he knew then that the other two were going to do him harm. He was going by a field of cabbage. "Oh," said he, "I am feeling bad, and I will go in here to die. Here are the bottles for you. Let me die here!"

It was well and it wasn't ill. They arrived home in great delight, and he never stopped or stayed until he came to his own country to the Queen of the Island of Loneliness, and he never went near the palace of the King of Ireland.

When he got home, his mother said, "Welcome home! I suppose you did good work while you were away."

"Yes," said he, "I did."

When he was with the Queen of the Well of Teentagh, he wrote a letter and laid it on her breast, saying that it was he, the son of the King of Ireland and the Queen of the Island of Loneliness, who had played that trick on her. So it went. When the Queen of the Well of Teentagh awoke, she saw the letter, and she read it and saw what was in it. There was no harm in that, and she paid no heed to it.

Time was passing then till it was past nine months, and, by dad, when the nine months were up, a son was born to her. And he was growing up, and when he was, off she went to the king and began to wage war and devastation on him, she and all her hosts, for she took all the men in the country with her.

One day when the King of Ireland's Son came in from hunting and harrying, his mother said to him, "Have you any news today?"

"I have not," said he. "Where would I get it? From the wild beasts of the forest or the birds of the air? But I know that you are not so."

"I am not, indeed," said she. "The Queen of the Well of Teentagh is waging war and devastation on the King of Ireland, and it is as well for you to get ready tomorrow and go to his aid."

"I will not!" said he.

"Oh, yes, you will!" said she, "for I will go with you! I will go along with you tomorrow," said she.

The Queen of the Island of Loneliness

It was well and it wasn't ill. The next morning, they got a ship ready. They never stopped or stayed until they came to land in the harbor—for there was a grand harbor there. And they drew up the ship and made for a regiment, the first regiment they saw, and they greeted them kindly, and, by dad, the others gave them not a greeting but a curse. "Attack those men and kill them, son!" said she. He began to slaughter them under him and over him on every side. Every man of the regiment who came near him was a dead man.

He did the same with the next regiment, and when that was done, he came up. And the queen had heard of the champion who had landed, and she asked the king had he any other son. He said he had, but that he had been killed in another country.

They made peace then, and when peace was made, they were talking together, and the Queen of the Island of Loneliness was talking to the King of Ireland and asked him where was his wife, and he said she was within the house. "Ask her to come out," said she, "and say that I wish to speak to her." She came out. "Oh," said the Queen, "here is a suit of clothes for you, for I wanted to bring you a present from my own country. Put them on," said she.

When she had put them on, the Queen said, "Squeeze!" and the suit squeezed.

"Who is the father of your elder son?" said the Queen.

"Oh, the King of Ireland," said she.

"Squeeze!" said the Queen, and the suit went on squeezing. "Now, who is his father?" said she.

"Oh!" said the other woman, "one day and I went out to

the gardener and he caught hold of me, and the older boy is his son."

It was well and it wasn't ill. She tried to take off the suit. "Squeeze!" said the Queen, and the suit went on squeezing. "Who is the father of your second son?" said she.

"Oh, the King of Ireland," said the other.

"Squeeze!" said the Queen. "Now, who is his father?"

"Oh, the King of Ireland," said she.

"Squeeze!" said the Queen to the suit, and the suit went on squeezing her. "Now, who is he?" said the Queen.

"Oh," said she, "one day I went into the bake-house, and the baker caught hold of me, and that boy is his."

The woman and the two boys were seized and brought out into the field, with five barrels of tar and five barrels of paraffin, and they were burnt to ashes.

It was well and it wasn't ill. "Now," said the Queen, "I can talk to the King of Ireland. Here is the son of the King of Ireland and the Queen of the Island of Loneliness." And she said to the Queen of the Well of Teentagh, "He will fight you for seven years, or if you prefer it, he will marry you. But he will fight you for seven years, if you like."

"Oh," said she, "I don't want to wage war or devastation on him, but only that he will marry me and come back with me to my own country."

By dad, the King of Ireland's Son and the Queen of the water of the Well of Teentagh were married, and he went over to the country where she lived, and he was king of the country of the water of the Well of Teentagh for the rest of his life, in the Queen's company. The Queen of the Island of Loneliness was married to the King of Ireland, and he brought her back to his own country, and they were together forever after. And that is my story.

the giant of the mighty blows

There was a time long ago, and it's long ago it was. If I'd been there then I wouldn't be here now. I'd have a new story or an old story or I'd be a gray-haired old storyteller. For there was a king in Ireland long ago. He had three sons, and they were growing up until they were about twenty years old. Then one day, by dad, the eldest said, "I'll not stay here any longer. I'll go abroad through the countries till I see what they are like, and I'll go hunting and harrying for myself."

And it was well and not ill. On the morrow morning he rose as early as the sun and set out, and he was traveling and traveling until the brightness of day was going from him and the darkness of night coming on him, the white nag going behind the dock-leaf, and *yeenach raw* from the dock-leaf, if she was waiting at all for him. He couldn't see sight of deer or damsel. "By dad," says he, "I'll be out all night."

He came to a wood, and when he did, "Well," says he, "the best place to hide myself is by going up into the wood until morning, and I'll pass the night." It was well and not ill. He went up into the wood and passed the night, and down he came in the morning, and he was shortening the road. He was traveling and traveling till late in the day, and, by dad, he saw a house in the distance, and it was far away. He made for it quick and lively, and when he did he came right into it. There was a little middle-aged man within.

"God save all here!" said the King of Ireland's Son.

"God and Mary save you!" said the man who was within.

"Well," said he, "I'm hungry, and you ought to get me food."

"Oh, I will," said he, "and welcome. Why wouldn't I?" He got him some food, and he ate well and had a fine meal. "How are you faring?" said the little man. "I need a man, and maybe you'd suit me?"

"Maybe, indeed," said the King of Ireland's Son. "I am wandering about looking for hire," said he. "That's the sort of man I am."

"Very good," said the little man. "By dad, maybe you'd suit me well!"

They made no bargain. "Any day," said he, "that you think I'm not paying you enough, you can go. And I have no great work to give you. Tomorrow morning I'll tell you what sort of work I have for you."

By dad, he got his supper all right, a fine supper, and a good bed to sleep on. The other man rose with dawn, and the King of Ireland's Son heard him and he got up, and when he was up the man had his breakfast ready for him. He ate a good breakfast.

"Now," said the man, "off with you!" He went out and let three small cattle out of the stable. "Now," said he, "drive these before you and give them grass, and bring them back here to me this evening."

"Very well," said the King of Ireland's Son.

He drove them before him. He was traveling till it was late

The Giant of the Mighty Blows

in the day, and he saw no place where he could stop with the cattle, where there was anything for them to eat. And he was driving the cattle before him, and, by dad, he came to a great wall-fence, and when he did, he looked in and there was fine grass inside, a big garden. He drew back from it and gave it a kick and a shoulder and knocked a great breach in the fence. When he did, he drove his small cattle in, and when he did, after a quarter of an hour he didn't know where the cattle were, except for the way they were trampling the grass and leaving a track behind them. By dad, he heard a storm coming, the bottom of the wood being thrown up and the top being thrown down, the old tree trembling and the young tree bending, with the storm that was made by a huge giant as he came from the Western World. That was a garden of his into which the King of Ireland's Son had driven the cattle. "Ah, by dad," said he, "that must be a great champion that is coming, and I had better stay out on the green lea, where the birds of the air and the wild beasts of the forest will see me."

He went out onto the green lea, and, by dad, a huge and horrible giant came up. "Oh," said he, "what shall I do with you, you ash-urchin from Ireland? Shall I put you like a pinch of snuff into one nostril and leave my other nostril empty, or blow you into the Eastern World, or put you seven miles under ground, where neither live man nor dead man will see you?"

"You ruffianly schemer," said the King of Ireland's Son, "don't you know that it's not to give you law or license that I came here, but to take law and license away from you?"

"Is that so?" said the giant.

"It is," said the King of Ireland's Son.

"Well, which do you prefer," said he, "to wrestle on bare hard red rocks or to fight with knives against ribs?"

"Oh, I'd sooner wrestle," said the King of Ireland's Son, "as I was used to do on the bouting-floor in Ireland."

With that they ran away from each other a quarter of a mile, and they ran toward each other, and they put an arm above and an arm below and an arm in true noble wrestling, till they were making soft ground of the hard ground and hard ground of the soft ground, and out of the gray rocks they were drawing spring-wells. Evening was coming on, and, by dad, he was not able to get the better of the giant.

The little robin came. "Oh, King of Ireland's Son," said she, "think of Ireland, and think of your people whom you left behind. And if the giant kills you," said she, "it will be a long day until I shall have covered you with a wisp of moss from bush, hole, and rock, and with the first gust of wind that comes," said she, "it will be blown away again. Let the blood of your little toe rise to the top of your head, and gaze no longer on the giant!"

With that, the blood of his little toe rose to the top of his head, and the blood of the top of his head went to his little toe. He gave the giant a thrust and drove him up to his knees into the ground, the second thrust up to his waist, the third thrust up to his Adam's apple. "Now," said he, "my fine giant, your head and your hold on life are mine!"

"Oh, they are," said the giant. "You are the best fighter

I have met from the setting to the rising of the sun. I have traveled east and I have traveled west and I have traveled every place, and in all that distance I have not seen a fighter as good as you. If you grant me my head and my hold on life, I'll give you a roan steed that will overtake the March wind ahead of her, and the March wind behind her will not overtake her. I'll give you a gold vessel and a silver vessel, and I'll give you a Sword of Light that can pierce any animal under the earth or over the earth, and I'll be your servant forever wherever you call on me."

"Where shall I find them?" said the King of Ireland's Son.

"Oh, you'll find them over there," said he. "There is a ring sticking up under that bush there, and lift up the ring and go down—put your finger in the ring and raise up the flagstone and go down there, and you'll find every one of them."

He raised up the flagstone then and went down into the hole, and the mare neighed so loudly that she was heard through the seven kingdoms. She thought he was going to take her out hunting and harrying. He took the sword and brought it up, and when he did, "Where shall I try it?" said he to the giant.

"Oh," said the giant, "try it on the root of that bush."

"Oh," said he, "I think that there is no root of a bush I'd rather try it on than the root of your own bush!" and he struck off his head and sent it whistling up—he sent it up into the air; and it was coming down again with a humming sound, and he gave it a kick and a shove and sent it seven hundred ridges and seven hundred rows out on the green lea.

"You did well!" said the giant. "If I had been able to get onto my body again, half the Fenians would not have cut me off again!"

"Oh, tell that to someone else!" said the King of Ireland's Son.

He went in then and began to search for his cattle in the garden, and he could not find them, but where the grass was trodden he was following the track. But even so he found them, and he drove them out and drove them home. And they had eaten so much that they were barely able to walk home. He came to the farmer and drove them into the stable, and they had plenty of milk.

He got a good supper, and he and the farmer were talking and discussing the world and the weather till it was bedtime. When it was, he got a good bed to sleep on, and when he did, "Be in no hurry rising," said the farmer, "until I call you in the morning. You'll be in time enough."

"Very well," said he.

Next morning the farmer was up good and early, and if he was, the King of Ireland's Son heard him and he got up. The farmer had his breakfast ready, and a good breakfast it was, and if it was, he ate it and went out. "Drive out your small cattle now," said he, "and give them grass, and bring them home to me in the evening."

"Very well," said the King of Ireland's Son.

He drove them off, and he was traveling and traveling until a long while of the day was spent, and he went by this garden and did not let them into it. He drove them a long way on and came to another big fence, and he looked in and

The Giant of the Mighty Blows

saw fine grass inside. And when he did he drew off from it. "Now," said he, "it would be a queer thing to say that I'd be driving my young beasts without their having anything since morning, and grass rotting in there." He drew off from it, and he gave it a kick and a shove and knocked down a big piece of it. And when he did, he drove in his small cattle. The grass was so high that it was as high as the best of the beasts. "By dad," said he, "they will go astray on me in there, and I'd better stand in front of them rather than let them go astray in the grass."

By dad, he had not them long inside when he heard the storm, so that the bottom of the wood was being sent to the top and the top to the bottom, the old tree was trembling and the young tree bending with the storm that a big giant was making as he came from the Eastern World. "Oh, by dad," said he, "I'd better go out on the green lea, where the birds of the air and the wild beasts of the forest will see me, rather than stay in here."

He went out on the green lea, and when he did, the big giant soon came up to him. "Oh, you ash-urchin from Ireland, what do you mean," said he, "by trampling my garden, and you after killing my brother? What shall I do with you, shall I put a pinch of snuff in one nostril and the other nostril empty, or blow you into the Eastern World or seven miles under ground where no man alive or dead will see you?"

"You ruffianly schemer," said the King of Ireland's Son, "it's not to give you law or license that I came here, but to take law and license away from you!"

"Is that so?" said the giant.

"It is," said the King of Ireland's Son.

"Well," said the giant, "which do you prefer, to wrestle on bare hard red rocks or to fight with knives against ribs?"

"Oh, I'd sooner wrestle," said the King of Ireland's Son, "as I was used to do on the bouting-floor in Ireland."

With that they ran away from each other a quarter of a mile, and then they ran toward each other, and they put an arm above and an arm below and an arm in true noble wrestling, till they were making soft ground of the hard ground and hard ground of the soft ground, and out of the gray rocks they were drawing spring-wells. By dad, the King of Ireland's Son—neither of them was able to get the better of the other.

The little robin came. "Oh," said she, "think of Ireland and of your people whom you left at home. And if the giant kills you," said she, "it is a long day till I shall have covered you with a wisp of moss from bush, hole, and rock, and with the first gust of wind that comes, it will be blown away again."

With that, the blood of his little toe rose to the top of his head, and the blood of the top of his head went to his little toe. He gave the giant a thrust and drove him into the ground up to his knees, the second thrust up to his waist, the third thrust up to his Adam's apple. "Now, my fine giant," said he, "your head and your hold on life are mine!"

"Oh, they are," said the giant. "You are the best fighter in the world," said he. "I have traveled east and west and north and south, and many is the great fighter I have killed, and you are the best man I have ever met! Now," said he, "if you grant me my head and my hold on life, I'll give you a crock

The Giant of the Mighty Blows

of gold and a crock of silver. I'll give you a Sword of Light that can pierce every animal under the earth or over the earth. And I'll give you a white steed," said he, "that will overtake the March wind ahead of her, and the March wind behind her will not overtake her."

"Where shall I find them?" said the King of Ireland's Son.

"There is a flagstone over there," said he, "and you'll find a ring in the stone. Put your finger in the ring, and the stone will rise up," said he, "and you will find them below."

He went over and he found the ring. He put his finger into the ring and raised the stone and went down. The horse neighed so that she was heard throughout the seven kingdoms, thinking that the warrior was coming to take her for hunting and harrying. He saw a crock of gold and a crock of silver there, as he had said, and he found the Sword of Light. He brought up the Sword of Light, and when he did, he said to the giant, "Where shall I try the edge of the blade?"

"Try it on the root of the bush over there," said the giant.

"Well," said he, "I think there is no root of a bush that I would rather try it on than the root of your own bush!" And he struck him where his head joined his neck, and sent his head into the air. The head was singing as it came down, but he leaped up, and as it turned to go back onto its body, he gave it a kick and a shove that sent it over seven ridges and seven rows out onto the green lea.

"You did well!" said the giant. "If I had got back onto my body, half the Fenians would not have cut me off again!"

"Oh," said the King of Ireland's Son, "you may tell that to someone else!"

He went on then to gather the small cattle, and there was no sign of them, except that he could follow the track in the grass that had been trampled, but even so he found them in the end. He drove his small cattle out and drove them home. He never stopped or stayed till he came home to the farmer, and when he did, he drove them into the stable; and they had eaten so much that they were hardly able to walk home.

By dad, the farmer had his supper ready for him, and they were conversing and talking and discussing the world and the weather until it was bedtime. Then the farmer said, "It is time for you to go to bed. I think you are tired after the day. Don't be in any hurry to get up in the morning until I call you and say that your breakfast is ready."

"Very well," said the King of Ireland's Son.

Next morning the farmer was up good and early, and if he was, the King of Ireland's Son got up, and he had his breakfast ready, a good breakfast; and he ate it and drove out his small cattle.

He was traveling and traveling till a good part of the day was spent. He went past those paddocks that he had seen the day before, and he did not see deer or damsel until he had walked a long way, and, by dad, at last he saw another paddock. He looked in on it, and he saw that there was grass in it half as high as the wall itself. "Oh," said he, "isn't it a great pity that my small cattle should be hungry, with so much grass in there!" He drew back and gave a kick and a shove to the wall and knocked a great breach in it.

He let in his small cattle, and the grass was as high as the cows themselves. "By dad," said he, "you will go astray. I had

The Giant of the Mighty Blows

better stand in front of you till you have eaten your fill!" And so he stood. He was standing in the high grass in the paddock, when he heard the storm coming, the bottom of the wood being sent to the top, and the top to the bottom, the old tree trembling and the young tree bending with the storm that a big giant was making as he came from the Eastern World. "Oh, by dad," said he, "this is no place for me. I had better go out onto the green lea, where the birds of the air and the wild beasts of the forest will see me!"

He went out onto the green lea, and soon a mighty giant came up to him. "Oh, you ash-urchin from Ireland," said he, "how did you dare to go trampling my paddock, after killing my two brothers in the last two days! What shall I do with you at all? Shall I put a pinch of snuff in one nostril and leave the other empty, or blow you into the Eastern World, or seven miles under ground where no man alive or dead will see you!"

"Oh," said the King of Ireland's Son, "it is not to give you law or license that I came here, but to take law and license away from you!"

"Is that so?" said the giant.

"It is!" said the King of Ireland's Son.

"Well," said the giant, "which do you prefer, to wrestle on bare hard red rocks or to fight with knives against ribs?"

"Oh, I'd sooner wrestle," said the King of Ireland's Son, "as I was used to do on the bouting-floor in Ireland."

With that they ran away from each other a quarter of a mile, and then they ran toward each other, and they put an arm above and an arm below and an arm in true noble wrestling, till they were making soft ground of the hard ground and hard ground of the soft ground, and out of the gray rocks they were drawing spring-wells. They did not know themselves which of them was the better or which the worse, and the sun was sinking in the west.

Then what should come but the little robin! "King of Ireland's Son," said she, "think of Ireland, and of your people whom you left at home, and if the giant kills you," said she, "it is a long day till I shall have covered you with a wisp of moss from bush, hole, and rock, and with the first gust of wind that comes, it will be blown away again."

With that, the blood of his little toe rose to the top of his head, and the blood of the top of his head went to his little toe. He gave the giant a thrust and drove him into the ground up to his knees, the second thrust up to his waist, and the third thrust up to his Adam's apple. "Now, my fine giant," said he, "your head and your hold on life are mine!"

"Oh, they are," said the giant, "and you are the best fighter from the setting sun to the rising sun. I have traveled east and I have traveled west, and I have traveled everywhere, and I never met a fighter whose head I did not cut off. Now, if you leave me my head and my hold on life I will give you a gray steed that will overtake the March wind ahead of her, and the March wind behind her will not overtake her. I will give you a Sword of Light that can pierce any animal that is under the earth or over the earth, and I will give you a crock of gold and a crock of silver, and I will be your servant wherever you call on me forever."

"Where shall I find those things?" said the King of Ireland's Son.

"There is a flagstone over there," said the giant, "and there is a ring in it. Put your finger in the ring and the flagstone will rise up, and there is not one of those things that you will not find down below."

He went over to the place as the giant told him, and he found the ring. He put his finger into the ring and raised the flagstone. He went down below, and the gray steed neighed so that she was heard throughout the seven kingdoms; and he saw the crock of gold and the crock of silver, and he saw the Sword of Light. He brought it up. "Where shall I try the edge of the blade?" said he to the giant.

"Try it on the root of a bush over there," said the giant.

"I think," said he, "that there is no root of a bush that I would rather try it on than the root of your own bush!" And he struck him where his head joined his neck and sent his head into the air. The head was singing as it came down, but he leaped up, and as it turned to go back onto its body, he gave it a kick and a shove that sent it over seven ridges and seven rows out onto the green lea.

"You did well!" said the giant. "If I had got back onto my body, half the Fenians would not have cut me off again!"

"Oh," said the King of Ireland's Son, "you may tell that to someone else!"

He went in and began to search for his small cattle, and found them at last out in the grass. He drove them out and along the road, and they had eaten so much that they were hardly able to walk, for it was splendid grass. And he drove them home to the farmer's house.

When he got there, the farmer had his supper ready. And,

as for milk, there wasn't a vessel in the farmer's house that was not full of milk. He had a good supper, and afterward they were talking and discussing the world and the weather till it was bedtime. "Now," said he to the King of Ireland's Son, "hurry off to bed, and don't be in any hurry to get up until I call you!"

He went to sleep and slept well that night, and next morning the King of Ireland's Son rose with the dawn. By dad, the farmer was up before him and had his breakfast ready! He ate a good breakfast, and then he drove out his cattle. "Bring out the cattle," said the farmer, "and give them plenty of grazing, and bring them home to me without any missing."

"Very well," said the King of Ireland's Son.

He drove them off, and he was traveling and traveling until high noon so that he might find a place where he could put in the cattle to graze. As he was driving them along, he came to a high wall, and he climbed onto it and looked in. When he looked in, he saw fine grazing there. "Isn't it a great pity," said he, "that my small cattle should be hungry with so much fine grass in there!" With that, he drew back and crashed against the wall with a kick and a shove so that he made a great breach in the fence. Then he let in his small cattle, and the grass was as high as themselves. "By dad," said he, "it would be better for me to stand inside and not to let you into the grass for fear it would cover you!"

It was well and it wasn't ill. He heard the storm, the bottom of the forest going to the top and the top to the bottom, the old tree breaking and the young tree bending in the storm that the giant made as he came from the Eastern World. It was

The Giant of the Mighty Blows

well. "By dad," said he, "I am in a bad place in here. Neither the birds of the air nor the wild beasts of the forest will see me. I had better go out onto the green lea."

He went out onto the green lea, and soon she came against him—the giants' mother!—a huge hag all covered with hair, the hair of her head down to her waist and the hair of her waist down to her feet. "Foo, faw, feet-yogue!" said the hag. "I smell the thieving Irishman who has killed my three sons in the last three days. But you won't succeed today, for I will take revenge on you! Which do you prefer, to wrestle on bare hard red rocks or to fight with knives against ribs?"

"Oh, I'd sooner wrestle," said the King of Ireland's Son, "as I was used to do on the bouting-floor in Ireland."

With that they ran away from each other a quarter of a mile, and then they ran toward each other, and they put an arm above and an arm below and an arm in true noble wrestling, till they were making soft ground of the hard ground and hard ground of the soft ground, and out of the gray rocks they were drawing spring-wells. Neither of them was getting the better of the other, and the hag's hair was so rough that it was taking the skin off him, and the sun was setting in the west.

The little robin came. "King of Ireland's Son," said she, "think of Ireland, and of your people whom you left at home, and if the giant kills you," said she, "it is a long day till I shall have covered you with a wisp of moss from bush, hole, and rock, and with the first gust of wind that comes, it will be blown away again."

With that, the blood of his little toe rose to the top of his head, and the blood of the top of his head went to his little toe. He gave the hag a thrust and drove her into the ground up to her knees, the second thrust up to her waist, the third thrust up to her neck. "Now, my fine giant," said he, "your head and your hold on life are mine!"

"Oh, they are," said the hag. "You are the best fighter in the world," said she. "I have traveled east and west and north and south, and many is the great fighter I have killed, and you are the best man I have ever met! Now," said she, "if you will grant me my head and my hold on life, I will give you a golden slingball which will kill whatever you throw it at, and it will come back into your hand."

"Where shall I find it?" said the King of Ireland's Son.

"Down in the corner of that wood under a big flagstone that is there!"

He went down and brought up the ball. "Where shall I test the power of your ball?" said he.

"On the ugliest tree you see in the forest," said she.

"I see no tree in the forest that is uglier than your own big tousled head!" said he, and threw the golden slingball at her, and the ball struck her in the mouth and passed out through the back of her head and killed her. He was tired then, and he went back to his cattle and brought them home.

His master had a great welcome for him, when he came home. He shook him by the hand. "You are the best herdsman I ever saw," said he. "I never sent a herdsman into that forest who was not killed, and my cattle never came home in their proper count."

When they had finished supper, they began talking and debating about the world and the weather, and the farmer asked him had he any news from the forest. He said he hadn't. "Where would I get news," said he, "where I had only the sky above my head and the wild birds and the forest around me?"

"Well, I have news," said the farmer.

"What is that?" said the King of Ireland's Son.

"The daughter of the king of this country is to be swallowed tomorrow by a dragon that will come in from the sea, unless a man can be found to save her. There will be great crowds meeting there. All the king's soldiers will be called in to save her; and she will be out there on the lawn below the palace, seated on a golden chair, with a silver chair beside her. It will be a great sight, and you must go to that meeting, and I will bring the cattle to the forest myself."

"I will not go there," said the King of Ireland's Son. "You go, and I will bring out the cattle to the forest, as I have done every day."

On the next day the King of Ireland's Son rose with the dawn, and the farmer was up before him and had his breakfast ready. He ate a good breakfast, and then he drove out his cattle, and the farmer went off to the meeting. When the cattle had eaten their fill, they lay down; and the King of Ireland's Son put on his battle dress and took the roan steed and the golden slingball. The roan steed went like the wind till she came to the place where the king's daughter was sitting. She rose up from the golden chair and bade him sit in it, and she sat in the silver chair beside him. He laid his head on her breast and told her, if she saw signs of anything coming over the sea, to take a hair from his head and that he would get up.

It wasn't long until the sea began to rise up into the sky, as the dragon came. The whole army was going into hiding in holes and hollows when they saw the dragon coming. They were frightened at the sight of it. The princess took a hair from his head, and he rose up. He threw the golden slingball at the dragon and wounded the dragon, and the ball came back to him. The dragon went around three times in the sea so that the whole sea was red with blood, and off it went.

The King of Ireland's Son sprang up and mounted his steed, and away he went. He never stopped or stayed till he came to where the cattle were. He put his horse in the stable, and the golden slingball with it, and he went home with his cattle.

The farmer was at home before him. They had supper then and began to talk. He asked the boy had he any news from the forest, and he said he hadn't. "Well, I have great news!" said the farmer.

"What is that?" said the boy.

"A great champion came today dressed like a young king in battle dress, with a golden slingball; and when the dragon came, he fired at it and wounded it, and it went away into the sea, and the princess tried to stop him, but he went off in spite of her. But the dragon is to come again tomorrow, and however it was today, it will be seven times worse tomorrow. The princess will surely be swallowed tomorrow unless there is someone to save her. You must go to the meeting tomorrow, and I will bring the cattle to the forest."

"I will not go," said the boy. "I came to you as a hired man, and I will go to the forest, as I went every other day."

In the morning, the King of Ireland's Son rose with the dawn. He ate his breakfast and went off to the forest with his cattle. The farmer went to the meeting, as he had gone the day before; and whatever excitement there was the first day, there was twice as much excitement around the princess on the second day. There were great crowds there.

When the cattle had eaten their fill, at about midday, the King of Ireland's Son put on his battle dress, and he brought his white steed and his golden slingball and set off like the wind and came to where the princess was sitting. She got up from the golden chair and gave it to him to sit in, and she sat in the silver chair beside him. He laid his head on her breast and told her, if she saw signs of anything coming over the sea, to take a hair from his head.

It was not long till the sea began to rise up, and howsoever the dragon was on the first day, it was five times worse on the second day. The whole army scattered in fear into every place where they could hide. The princess took a hair from his head. He jumped up and threw his golden slingball at the dragon, and sent it into its mouth and out through its side, and he killed it with the golden ball, and the ball came back into his hand again. He jumped up and sprang into the saddle; and she tried to stop him, but she was able only to take one of the slippers he was wearing, and he escaped from her. [The storyteller may have omitted a third fight, to which the hero comes on the gray steed. Only two of the three horses appear here in the rescue.]

She fell into a sick sadness then for love of the young king who had saved her from the dragon. She was carried into the palace and put into her own room with twelve doctors attending her.

The King of Ireland's Son went back to the forest. He put his white steed into the stable and hid his battle dress and his golden slingball. He came home in the evening, and the farmer was at home before him. They ate their supper, and then the farmer asked him had he any news from the forest. He said he hadn't. "Well, I have news," said the farmer. "The dragon came again today, and a king's son came and killed it; and the princess is sick, with twelve doctors attending her. She fell into a sick sadness for the young king when he left her, and she was able only to take one of his slippers. The king has made a proclamation throughout the kingdom. Everyone, high and low, from the poor man to the landlord, and from the king to the beggar, must come to try on the slipper, and whomsoever the slipper fits, that is the man the princess needs to bring her back to health. There will be a great sight to be seen there tomorrow, and you must go there, and I will bring the cattle to the forest myself."

"I will not go," said he. "It was not for that that I was hired."

Next morning, the King of Ireland's Son rose with the dawn. He ate his breakfast and went off to the forest as he had done each day. As soon as the farmer had got up and had his breakfast, he went off to the meeting that was gathered around the king's palace. There were four noblemen going round with the slipper, and whosoever could wear the slipper was the man that was wanted. Some were cutting off their toes and others were cutting off their heels in hope that the slipper might fit them, but it was no use. The slipper was not fitting any one of them. The old king was asking everyone then did they know of anyone they had left behind at home who was not at the meeting. This man who had the boy said that he had a boy at home, looking after the cattle, and that he was always asking him to come to the meeting, but he would not come. Four soldiers were sent then to fetch him, but he would not come.

When the soldiers went off, after an hour or so, the King of Ireland's Son saw on the road a poor stooping man with a bag on his back and a stick in his hand, dressed all in rags. He went up to the poor man and told him he would exchange clothes with him and give him the clothes he was wearing.

"Don't make fun of me like that!" said the man.

"It is not fun at all," said he. "What does it matter to you, so long as I give you my clothes?" He took off his clothes and gave them to the poor man, and the poor man gave his own clothes to him. "Give me the bag that is on your back, and the stick in your hand!" said he. The poor man gave them to him.

The King of Ireland's Son went off then to the palace and stood outside the gate, bent and bowed. The four noblemen were there, and they had tried the slipper on every man that was there. "Have you tried it on the poor old man who is outside the gate?" said the old king.

"We have not," said they. He told them to go and try the slipper on him. They went up to him and told him to stretch out his foot.

"Sure, you would not ask the like of me to put my foot near a shoe of that sort?" said he.

"You will have to stretch out your foot," said they, "for it is the law."

As soon as he stretched out his foot, the slipper jumped out of their hands and went up onto his foot. The noblemen took him and carried him on their shoulders into the palace and up into the room where she was sleeping, with twelve doctors attending her. As soon as she got sight of him, she jumped out of bed and put her arms around him and kissed him. "The man for love of whom I am dying," she said, "the man who saved me from the dragon out of the sea, is mine at last!"

A king's clothes were put on him at once. They went to church and were married, and they had a wedding that lasted for seven weeks, with eating and drinking and sport and pleasure for them and for everyone that came that way. The old king gave half his kingdom to the King of Ireland's Son until the day of his death, and the whole kingdom from that day forward. When the old king died, he had the whole kingdom.

the knowledge of the only story and the dúdán's sword

There was a king in Ireland long ago, and he was (happily) married to a young queen. It was well and it wasn't ill. The queen died, and he had a young son, and if so, by dad, the son was growing up until he came to be twelve years old. And when he was twelve years old, the king's counselors came to him—the highest leaders—and they asked him what he was doing, spending his life as he was, and he said that he would not put a stepmother over his son, and that he was loth to marry. By dad, they went to him and talked this way and that way, saying that, if he built a great castle and sent the boy to live in it, the young queen he might marry would not know that he was married before.

It was well and it wasn't ill. He began to build the castle, and he spent seven years building it, and when he had spent seven years building the castle, it was ready and finished, and he put every sort of furniture that he could find into the great castle, and he put in a young nurse to take care of the boy, and he put in everything that the boy would need.

He had his hurley-stick and his ball, and he used to be striking under him and over him any day he cared to go out, when the nurse would let him out; and without that, he could not go out. All was well, and he was growing up, and then the young king married and got another queen, and the queen did not know that he had ever been married before.

It was well and it wasn't ill. The boy was growing up till he was twenty years old, and when he was, one day then, a fine sunny day, he said to the nurse, "Well, it's fine today, and you ought to let me out to play ball."

"Oh," said she, "maybe it would be better for you to stay where you are."

"Oh," said he, "the day is fine, and let me out, when I ask you."

It was well, and she let him out, and he began striking under him and over him at the ball, and, by dad, he drove it out over the gate, and he had to go in to ask the nurse for the key of the gate. She gave him the key, and he went out, and when he did, what should he find outside but a little middle-aged man, a farmer; and "God save you!" said the farmer.

"God save you kindly!" said the King of Ireland's Son. "You know me, and I don't know you!"

"I know you," said the farmer. "King of Ireland's Son, would you play a game of cards?"

"Well," said the King of Ireland's Son, "I don't know. I never refused any sort of pastime yet."

They began to play hard and very hard, and, by dad, the King of Ireland's Son won the game. "Now lay your *geasa*!" said the farmer.

"I put you under *geasa* of heavy magic," said he, "not to sleep two nights in the same bed nor to eat two meals at the same table till you bring me the loveliest woman in the world."

"Very well," said the farmer. "I'll have her for you in a week's time."

It was well. He went back into the courtyard, and after a week he went out again and began to strike the ball under him and over him. And, if he did, he drove it out of the yard again, and he went in to ask for the key, and they had to let him out. What should he find outside, but the farmer with the loveliest woman that ever sun or wind played on.

"Oh," said the King of Ireland's Son, "have you found her?"

"Indeed I have," said he. "Why not? Here she is for you!"

He gave her to him, and when he did, he brought her into the palace. And so it was. He was very comfortable, very comfortable altogether. He had a fine young lady, and for a whole month he never wanted to go out at all!

By dad, after a month he said to the nurse—he came to his senses that day—"You ought to let me out today to play ball. The day is fine and you ought to let me out."

"Maybe," said the nurse, "it would be better for you to stay where you are."

Even so, he kept at her till she gave him the ball and let him out. And he began striking under him and over him, and he was not long striking until he drove the ball out over the gate. And when he drove it out over the gate, he went in again to get the key, and they had to let him out. And then who was outside waiting for him but the farmer!

"God save you, King of Ireland's Son!" said the farmer. "How do you like the young woman?"

"Very well," said the King of Ireland's Son.

"Would you play a game of cards, King of Ireland's Son?" said he.

"By dad, I will!" said the King of Ireland's Son. "Why wouldn't I?"

It was well and it wasn't ill. They played hard and very hard, and as they played, the farmer won. "Now," said the King of Ireland's Son, "what are your *geasa*?"

"Oh," said he, "you'll hear them soon enough! I put you under *geasa* of heavy magic not to sleep for two nights in the same bed nor to eat two meals at the same table until you bring me the Knowledge of the Only Story and the Dúdán's Sword!"

"Very well," said the King of Ireland's Son.

In he went. He had that night left, and that was all he had. In he went, and when he went in, he sat down and the chair broke under him. "Oh!" said the nurse, "I knew well that you would do no good out there!"

"What harm?" said he. "There is no harm done."

On the following morning, the King of Ireland's Son rose as early as the dawn, and, by dad, the young lady was up and had his breakfast ready. It was well and it wasn't ill. He set out. He stood on his left leg and turned onto his right leg and asked God to send him safe. Out he went, and away, and he was traveling then until well on in the day. He did not see sign of deer or damsel. He was traveling and ever traveling until the bright light of day was going from him, the darkness of night coming toward him, the white nag going behind the dock-leaf, and *yeenach raw* from the dock-leaf, if it was waiting at all for him, and if it was waiting there he didn't care. By dad, he saw a little light in the distance, and it was far away. "I always heard," said he to himself, "in the olden days when I went through the book, if you should see a light at the fall of night, and if darkness should take it away from you, half the Fenians would not find it again." He made for it quick and lively and came up to it at the dark black fall of night.

He knocked at the door, and when he knocked, an old gray-haired man rose out of the corner and opened the door, and when he had opened the door, he shook hands with the King of Ireland's Son.

"Oh," said he, "you know me, and I don't know you at all!"

"Oh, I know you," said the farmer. He was so old that his bones were nearly out through his skin. It was well. He gave him a chair. The chair broke under him. "Ah," said he, "you are a king's son under *geasa*. Would it be any harm for me to ask what *geasa* are upon you?"

"Not at all," said the King of Ireland's Son. He told him the story as I have told it to you.

"Oh," said he, "I don't know what to say to you, but I have no information to give you. Tomorrow night you will meet a brother of mine, and he may have information to give you."

By dad, it was well. They spent a third of the night with Fenian tales, a third with folktales, and a third (in discussing the world and the weather), until it was time to go to bed, as the farmer told about every adventure he went through during his life. He got a good bed to lie on and a good supper. "Now," said the farmer, "don't be in any hurry to get up until I wake you in the morning."

It was well and it wasn't ill. At the dawn of day, he heard the farmer already up, and he got up. The farmer had his breakfast ready for him, and a good breakfast it was. "Now," said the farmer, "you will meet a brother of mine tonight. I will give you a horse, and when you reach his gate, tie the reins to the saddle and turn the horse, and he will come back home to me."

It was well and it wasn't ill. Away with him; he mounted the horse and was gone. He took hills with a leap and hollows with a jump. He overtook the March wind ahead of him, and the March wind behind him did not overtake him. Soon it was midday, and he could not see sight of deer or damsel. "I shall make no distance today," said he to himself.

He was traveling and ever traveling till the brightness of the day was going from him, the darkness of night coming toward him, the white nag going into the shadow of the dockleaf, and *yeenach raw* from the dock leaf, if it would wait at all for him; and he saw a little light in the distance, and it was far away. "I always heard," he said, "if you should see a light at the fall of night, and if darkness should take it away from you, half the Fenians would not find it again."

He reached it by nightfall, and he did with the horse as the farmer had told him and turned it for home, and as soon as he had turned it, away went the horse.

He knocked at the door and went in. As old as the other farmer was, this man was seventeen times as old. His bones were breaking with age. He shook hands with the King of Ireland's Son, and when he did, your man said, "You know me, and I don't know you."

"Oh, I know you," said the old man. "Why wouldn't I?" He gave him a chair, and, by dad, the chair broke under him. "Oh," said he, "you are a king's son under *geasa*. Would it be any harm to ask what *geasa* are on you?"

"None at all," said the King of Ireland's Son.

He told him the story as I have told it to you, and when he had told it, the farmer said, "I don't know what to say to you, but this much—tomorrow night you will meet a brother of mine, and he will have more information to give you."

It was well. He gave him a good supper, and they were talking about the world and the weather till it was time to go to bed. "Don't be in any hurry to get up in the morning," said he, "until I call to you that breakfast is ready." Next morning at the break of day, the King of Ireland's Son was very anxious; and he turned in bed and heard the farmer already up. When he heard that, he got up, and the poor farmer treated him well. He had breakfast ready for him. When he had finished, he went out, and he stood on his left leg and turned onto his right leg, and asked God to send him safe. "Well now, don't go yet," said the farmer. "I will give you a horse, and you will tie the reins to the saddle, when you reach my brother ["him" in text]. You will surely reach him by nightfall, and make no delay, but turn the horse, and he will come back home to me."

It was well and it wasn't ill. He was traveling and ever traveling. He was taking the hills with a leap and the hollows with a jump till the brightness of the day was going from him, the darkness of night coming on him, the white nag going into the shadow of the dock-leaf, and *yeenach raw* from the dock-leaf, if it would wait at all for him. He saw a little light in the distance and it was far away, as the dark twilight of night came on. When he did, he made for it quick and lively, and, by dad, he reached it at the dark black fall of night. He did with the horse as the farmer told him and turned it for home; and when he did, away went the horse.

When he knocked at the door, the farmer stood up, and he was the oldest of them, and as he was the oldest of them, there was no telling his age. He shook hands with him and said, "A hundred thousand welcomes, King of Ireland's Son!"

"Oh, long life to you!" said the King of Ireland's Son. "You know me, and I don't know you."

"Oh, I know you," said the farmer. "Why wouldn't I?" said he.

It was well and it wasn't ill. He gave him a chair, and the chair broke under him. When the chair broke, he said, "You are a king's son under *geasa*! Would it be any harm to ask what *geasa* are on you?"

"None at all," said your man, and he told him.

"Oh!" said he "that is a magician and he could kill the whole world. There is no describing him! I don't know what to say to you. That man has the power of magic and enchantment, and there is no describing him. But there is this much," said he. "He has been away in the Western World for seven months and seven days, and he should be back by now."

By dad, he got supper ready, a good supper, and they ate it

together. When they had finished, "Now," said he, "don't be in any hurry getting up until I call you in the morning."

"Very well," said the King of Ireland's Son.

By dad, he slept well that night, and in the morning he got up and ate his breakfast. "Now," said the farmer, "it is time for you to go to him. He is not far from you. He is in such and such a place," said he, "and I will give you a horse. Go to his palace, riding on the horse, and go around the palace till you come in front of the entrance, and he is within in a room beyond the door. The door is open and the room is within beyond it, and he is asleep on the bed. And the sword," said he, "his hand is holding the sword, and if he is awake, his eyes are shut, and if he is asleep, his eyes are open."

By dad, it was well. "Then," said he, "when you have come around the palace and you are in front of the entrance, shout out loud and tell him to send out the Knowledge of the Only Story and the Dúdán's Sword. Press your horse, and make no delay in jumping the gate, or else you are a dead man!"

By dad, he did as the farmer told him, and went around the palace till he came in front of the entrance, and when he was in front of the entrance, he called on the wizard to send out at once the Knowledge of the Only Story and the Dúdán's Sword. And he took his horse to the gate, and he was just above the gate, and the wizard struck the horse on the hindquarters, and half the horse fell inside and half fell outside, and the King of Ireland's Son suffered no harm. The wizard had cut the horse in two, so that one half fell inside and the other half fell outside!

He came home to the farmer. "Oh!" said the farmer, "you

have done very well." It was well and it wasn't ill. "Stay here till tomorrow night!" said he. And so it was, until the next day.

Next morning he got him another horse. "Do the same thing again!" he said. "Go and ride around the palace again, and tell him, when you come in front of the entrance, to send out the Knowledge of the Only Story and the Dúdán's Sword. And press on with your horse to the gate, and unless you get past the gate, you are a dead man!"

It was well and it wasn't ill. When he was just above the gate, the horse was struck again so that half of it was left inside and the other half outside. Off he went. He had fallen outside, with half of the horse, and the other half lay within. And he went off home. He had no horse. The horse was dead. He never stopped or stayed till he came home to the farmer. When he came home to the farmer, he said, "You have done very well."

It was well and it wasn't ill—I may as well shorten it—till he had killed the ninth horse—there is no use in following it through—till he had killed nine horses, and the ninth was killed, half of it inside and half outside—do you see, I would make it too long, following through to the end, but I am doing well.

"You have done very well," said the farmer. "Now," said he—that was the tenth day—"he was seven months and seven days in the Western World, and he has been so long, and nine months and nine days since he came back; and he has been awake all that time without sleeping a wink. Now," said he, "go to him tomorrow, and don't mind about a horse before-

Knowledge of the Only Story and the Dúdán's Sword 89

hand. He is in his room. Come to the door as quietly as ever you can, and look in; and if he is asleep, his eyes are open, and if he is awake, his eyes are shut."

It was well and it wasn't ill. He went to the door as quietly as ever he could and looked in. "By dad, you are asleep!" said he. He heard him snoring. Every snore he gave (was drawing in the two sides of the house). In he went, and the sword was in the wizard's hand—his hand was open, and the big sword lay in his hand. The farmer had said, "Get hold of the sword if you can, and jump back, if you can take the sword from him, and warn him to keep clear or you will cut off his head!"

He did as the farmer had told him [here the narrator went back a little in his story but made no change] and he never stopped or stayed till he came to the door, and he looked in, and when he looked in, he saw him inside, and he was asleep! In he went. He never stopped or stayed till he was inside, and he caught hold of the sword and jumped away.

"You ruffianly schemer, you ash-urchin from Ireland," said the wizard. "I'll cut off your head!"

"Oh," said the King of Ireland's Son, "keep clear, or it is I who will cut off *your* head! I will cut off your head at once unless you tell me the Knowledge of the Only Story!"

"Well," said the wizard, "I will tell you the Knowledge of the Only Story right to the end. You want the Knowledge of the Only Story, and you have the Dúdán's Sword. That is the Dúdán's Sword in your hand, and now I will tell you the Knowledge of the Only Story."

He sat down, and when he was seated, "Now," said he, "I was east and I was west. I was in the Western World and I was in the Eastern World. I have spent my life fighting and killing. And one day—I had a grandmother, an old, old woman—I did something that vexed her, and she struck me with a magic rod and turned me into a cock! And there I was for seven years running amongst all the hens. I spent seven years running amongst all the hens, and when the seven years were up she turned me into a man again.

"It was well and it wasn't ill. Time passed for another seven years, and I did something again that vexed her, and when I did, she got the magic rod again and struck me and turned me into a bull. And I was bulling all the cows for seven years. When the seven years were up, she made me a man again, and then I was a man, as I had been before. By dad, I did something again to vex her, and what should she do but turn me into a great big dog! Then I was for seven years a dog, as big as a cow's calf, with a big chain on me. There I was, and I did not know in the world what to do.

"One day, I was outside. I was watching her, and I saw her putting the magic rod under her pillow. I knew then where she kept the magic rod. There was a house outside where there was a little child. She was gone hunting and harrying for herself to the Eastern World or to the Western World, as often she was, with magic and enchantment. While she was away, I brought the little boy to the door, and I got the magic rod and threw it on the ground beside me. The boy took it up and had it in his hand, and then I caught him by the arm and put my teeth into his arm so as to make him strike me with the rod. He did not strike me. I let his arm free. There I was for two hours trying to make the boy strike me with the magic rod!

After a while, he gave me a little blow with the magic rod, and turned me into a man. I hid the magic rod then in a place where she has never found it since!

"Well now," said he, "there you have the Knowledge of the Only Story, and you have the Dúdán's Sword. Do you know," said he, "who sent you here in search of the Knowledge of the Only Story and the Dúdán's Sword?"

"No," said the King of Ireland's Son.

"The Goblin sent you! That is who sent you here! Now, when you go home, he will be there to meet you; and he will be on the lookout so that he may know when you arrive home. He will welcome you home, and he will ask you have you got it; and say that you have. Then tell him the Knowledge of the Only Story, and hand him the Dúdán's Sword, for you are bound to hand it to him. He will give a roar that will be heard throughout the seven kingdoms, and he will be so joyful and triumphant on account of the sword that it will fall from his hands. Seize it at once and cut off his head, or else you are a dead man!"

It was well and it wasn't ill. He and that great churl shook hands, and he bade him good-bye. Away with him, and he never stopped until he came to the farmer. The farmer shook hands with him and bade him welcome. "Ah," said the farmer, "you are a great fellow! You have done very nicely, and indeed I thought that you had no chance." He got him a good supper, and they had great conversation until it was time to go to bed; and when it was time, he got a good bed to sleep on. "Sleep as long as you like now," said he, "until morning, and I will have your breakfast ready for you." It was well. He slept as long as he liked. At break of day, he was uneasy. He got up, and the farmer was up before him and had his breakfast ready. "Now," said he, "I will give you a horse, and you will reach my brother tonight, and all you need do with the horse is as you did before."

He set his horse to a gallop, and he was traveling and ever traveling till the bright light of the day was going from him, the darkness of night coming toward him, the white nag going behind the dock-leaf, and *yeenach raw* from the dock-leaf, if it would wait at all for him. By dad, he saw a light in the distance, and it was far away. "I always heard," said he to himself, "if you saw a light at the fall of night, and darkness should take it away, that half the Fenians would not find it." He came up to it at the dark black fall of night. He knocked at the door and went in to the farmer, and the farmer shook him by both hands, and gave him a hundred and a thousand welcomes.

"By dad," said he, "you have done very well, and indeed I thought that I would never see you again!"

"Oh, well," said your man, "I have done well. I have indeed."

He gave him a good supper, and then they were talking about the world and the weather until it was bedtime, and he gave him a good bed to sleep on. He slept well that night and very well, and in the morning he rose with the sun, and the farmer was up before him and had his breakfast ready. "Now," said the farmer, "eat your breakfast, and I will give you a horse, and you will reach my brother tonight." That was the third brother on his journey home. "By dad," said he, "do with the horse as you did before. Tie the reins to the saddle, and turn the horse for home, and it will come back here to me."

Off with him then, and he was traveling and ever traveling till the brightness of day was going from him, the darkness of night coming toward him, the white nag going behind the dock-leaf, and *yeenach raw* from the dock leaf, if it would wait at all for him. And late in the evening, by dad, he saw a little light in the distance, and it was far away. "I always heard," said he to himself, "if you saw a light at the fall of night, and darkness should take it away, that half the Fenians would not find it." He came up to it at the dark black fall of night, and there he did with the horse as the farmer had told him and knocked at the door and went in.

The farmer shook him by both hands and gave him a hundred and a thousand welcomes. "By dad," said he, "you have done very well, and I thought I would never see you again!"

"I have," said your man.

He gave him a good supper, and they were talking about the world and the weather until it was bedtime; and then he gave him a good bed to sleep in. "Now," said he, "tomorrow morning be in no hurry to get up. I will have your breakfast ready for you in the morning, and I will give you a horse that will bring you home to your own palace gate."

He slept well that night, and very well, and in the morning he got up, and, by dad, the farmer was up before him! He had breakfast ready, a good breakfast, and he ate it. Then he gave him a horse. "Now," said he, "ride off, and you will reach your own gate at such and such a time today, and then do with the horse as you did before, and turn her for home, and the horse will come back home to me."

Away he went! He traveled along, and it was late in the evening when he reached the gate. He turned the horse for home and tied the reins to the saddle, and away went the horse back to the farmer.

In he went then, and he had the sword in his hand, and who should be waiting for him inside the gate but the Goblin ["farmer" in the text]. "God save you, King of Ireland's Son," said the Goblin. "You have come back!"

"Yes," said the King of Ireland's Son.

"Have you got it?" (said the Goblin).

"Oh, I have," said the King of Ireland's Son. He told him the Knowledge of the Only Story as I have told it to you, and then handed him the sword, and the Goblin ["he" in the text] gave a shout, and the shout he gave was heard throughout the seven kingdoms—and, by dad, the sword fell out of his hand!

Then the King of Ireland's Son sprang forward and took the sword and struck him in the neck and sent his head whistling into the air. And then it was humming coming down and tried to go back onto its body again. And he sprang forward and gave it a kick and a shove and sent it seven hundred ridges and seven hundred rows out onto the green lea.

"Oh, you did well!" said the Goblin ["farmer" in the text]. "If you had not done that, I would have done as much to you."

"Oh, tell that to someone else!" said the King of Ireland's Son.

He went off then into the house. And when he went in, the

young lady shook hands with him and he gave her a kiss, and she did not know how to do enough for him, and that was no blame to her. And he lived in comfort for the rest of his life as long as his life lasted.

terror without fear

There was a king in Ireland long ago, and he had a son, and the son's name was Terror without Fear. When he was twenty-one years of age, he set out and turned toward the sea and went to the brink of the beach. A coracle came in to him from the rough sea in which there was only one man.

"God bless you, son of the king," said he, "Terror without Fear!"

"God and Mary to you!" says Terror without Fear. "You recognize me, and I do not recognize you!"

"You would not fail to recognize people, but that you never left your father's demesne and court till today. Son of the king," says he, "would you play a game of cards?"

"Yes, but I have not brought my gaming things with me from home."

"I am the man," said he, "that never went outside the door, onto hill or hillock, on land or sea, without having my pack of cards with me"—drawing his gray-green table out of the bridge of his nose, his golden chair and his chair of silver. "Son of the king," said he, "why don't you sit in the chair of gold?"

"I will not," said the king's son, "for I have not even a silver chair at home."

They began to play, and the king's son played so that he won twenty-one games against him.

"Son of the king," said he, "lay your *geasa*!"

"I put you," said the king's son, "under *geasa* of heavy magic and under the great censure of the year, from the kitchen door to the farthest part from me of the land—of my father's land—that space to be filled with cattle, small and big, and that they may never be taken from me."

"My curse on you," said he, "Terror without Fear. You have made me poor forever!"

"When I get home," said Terror without Fear, "and tell whom I had to do with, I shall want to know his name."

"You will call him," said he, "you will say," says he, "that it is Second Rod without Tidings whom you had to do with. But will you come tomorrow?" says he.

"Yes," said the king's son.

He went home well pleased. He saw cattle of every kind grazing when he arrived. He made haste to climb a hill. He looked in every direction and saw them.

"Well, father," said he, "come out to see what I have as a result of this day."

"They are yours today," said his father, "and they will be gone tomorrow!"

"Oh, father," said he, "they shall not! I made a binding agreement."

He ate his supper and went to sleep until the next morning. He arose at dawn, looked out, and saw the cattle just as they were the evening before. He only ate his breakfast and set out down the same path by which he had gone the day before till he came to the brink of the beach. He was only just standing there when he saw the coracle coming in from the sea.

"God bless you, son of the king!" said he. "You are pleased with yesterday."

"Yes," said the king's son, "and perhaps I may be as pleased with today."

He draws out his gray-green table, his golden chair, and his chair of silver, and it was under the lids of his two eyes that he had them. The king's son just sat in the silver chair.

"Son of the king," said he, "why would you not sit in the golden chair?"

"I will not," said the king's son, "for I have not even a silver chair at home."

He laid out his pack of cards. The king's son won twenty-one games against him again.

"Son of the king," said he, "lay your *geasa*."

"I will," said he, "for I worked for it. I put you under *geasa* of heavy magic and under the great censure of the year, to make a town within half a mile of my father's court, a river to be flowing through the middle of it, and half of it on each side, and people selling and buying there; and everyone, when he sees me coming, that they shall say to themselves that they must be selling smartly, for the master is coming—and that it may never be taken from me."

"Oh, my curse on you, Terror without Fear! You have made me poor forever!" He arose and took away his gray-green table, his golden chair, and his chair of silver. "Son of the king," said he, "will you come tomorrow?"

"Yes," said the king's son.

He went home. He stood on the top of the hill. He saw before him the town, the river flowing through the middle of it, women and children coming and going.

"By dad," said he, "you are all right anyhow. Mother," said he, "get ready my supper for me! You shall be able to go into your town tomorrow to fetch whatever you want. It is mine," said he, "and the day it is mine, it is yours as well."

On the morning of the third day he arose at dawn. He washed his face, his eyes and eyebrows, he asked God to prosper him. "If I come safe," said he, "that is all the card playing I shall do forever."

He went down by the same path till he came to the brink of the beach. He was only just standing there when he saw the floating coracle coming toward him over the sea.

"Oh, God bless you, son of the king," said he, "Terror without Fear! You are pleased with yesterday."

"Maybe," said the king's son, "I'll be just as pleased with today."

"Maybe," said he.

He set down on the ground his gray-green board, his golden chair, and his chair of silver, and the place he took them from was the whites of his eyes. The king's son just took the silver chair and sat in it.

"Oh, son of the king," said he, "why will you not sit in the golden chair?"

"I won't sit in it," said the king's son, "for I haven't even a silver chair at home."

He won twenty-one games against Second Rod without Tidings again on the third day.

"Terror without Fear," says he, "lay your *geasa!*"

"I will," said he, "because I worked for it. I put you under *geasa* of heavy magic and under the great censure of the year to set the loveliest woman that was ever under water or over water, under land or over land, at my right side as I go home, and that she may never be taken away from me. But I have played my last game with you forever."

"You have her now," said he, "but even so it is her own fortune you have with her. She is the loveliest woman that was ever under water or over land. Her name is the Furious Flame, and may you not live to enjoy her!"

He looked behind him. The young lady was beside him, and she smiled at him. He took both her hands in his. He smothered her with kisses. He drowned her with tears. He dried her with silk napkins and the hair of her own head.

He came home. He struck the challenge-pole. The challenge-pole screamed so that poor and naked, high and low assembled, and they held a wedding for seven nights and seven days of joy and pleasure for himself and the Furious Flame.

On the eighth day after he married, he set out to go to town. He saw a man approaching, and he came up to him. "God bless you, Terror without Fear!"

"God and Mary to you!" said Terror without Fear. "You know me and I do not know you."

"You will soon know me," said he. "My name is Iron Waist. I have come to you so that wherever you put your foot, I may put my two feet, wherever you put your hand, I may put my two hands, so that you may never call me by any other name than brother and that I may do the same to you!"

"Is that what you came for?" said Terror without Fear.

"That is why I came," said Iron Waist.

He went back home and brought him with him. He came in to his father, his mother, and his wife. "Here is a comrade that I have brought and a brother as well." The father and the mother and the wife got up, and they said that they had never seen anything that pleased them better, provided that they could get it from him in writing. Iron Waist said that he would give it in writing with a thousand welcomes. They were in and out together then for a week.

"Well," said Terror without Fear, when the week was up—Terror without Fear said to Iron Waist that they would go hunting that day.

Iron Waist said that they need not both go. "I will go hunting," said he, "but do you stay to take care of your wife."

"No," said Terror without Fear. "We shall go together."

They had gone only a mile and a half over the mountain, when the three Sharachauns (that means "giants") came from their crimson country and carried off the young lady through the roof of the house. "Well," said they, "we have the loveliest woman that was ever under water or over water, under ground or over ground, whichever of the three of us is to get her."

They carried her off to Gleann Tuirc to the king, so that he should decide among them about the woman. The name of the king they came to was Fionn Mhac Cumhaill.

The three Sharachauns came in. Fionn asked them where they were going. "For you to decide," said they, "about this woman, which man of us is to have her."

"Who is she?" said Fionn.

"She is the wife of Terror without Fear," said they, "the loveliest woman that moon or sun ever shone on, the Furious Flame, daughter of Second Rod without Tidings."

"What is your name?" he said to the first man who came in.

"You may call me the Greedy Sharachaun," said he.

"What is your name?" he said to the second man.

"You may call me the Simple Sharachaun," said he.

"What is your name?" he said to the third man.

"The Gloomy Sharachaun," said he.

"Well, Greedy Sharachaun," said he, "how old are you?"

"I was seven years here and seven years yonder, and I was seven years traveling. I brought with me a full boatload of razors. I never gave one, and I never sold one, and I haven't a razor left today to lay on my cheek!"

"How old are you?" said he to the Simple Sharachaun.

"I was seven years here and seven years yonder, and I was seven years traveling. I brought with me a full boatload of pipes. I never gave one, and I never sold one, and I haven't a pipe left today that I could smoke!"

"You are fairly old," said he. "Well, Gloomy Sharachaun," said he, "how old are you?"

"I was seven years here and seven years yonder, and I was seven years traveling. I brought with me a full boatload of forks. I never gave one, and I never sold one, and I haven't a fork left today to put a bit of food in my mouth!"

"Well, Greedy Sharachaun, what is the greatest laziness that ever came on you?"

"Well," said the Greedy Sharachaun, "if I were in a house of lead, and the four corners of the house caught fire, laziness would prevent me from getting up from where I lay."

"Simple Sharachaun, what is the greatest laziness that ever came on you?"

"Oh, master," said he, "if I were sitting on a rock by the sea, and the tide were rising over me, laziness would prevent me from moving before I was drowned."

"You are fairly lazy," said he.

"Gloomy Sharachaun," said he, "what is the greatest laziness that ever came on you?"

"Oh, master," said he, "the loveliest woman that ever moon or sun shone on is here with us, and if I were lying in bed with her till morning, if I were turned away from her, laziness would prevent me from turning to her till morning."

"Well," said Fionn, "you shall have the woman."

"Well," said Goll, "I will fight for the woman rather than let her go."

"Will you fight Goll?" said Fionn to the Gloomy Sharachaun.

"Upon my soul, I will not," said the Gloomy Sharachaun. And the three Sharachauns went off again, leaving the woman with Goll.

When Terror without Fear came home in the evening with his comrade Iron Waist, he found his father over a basin which he had filled with tears and his mother beyond him in the same state. He asked his father what was wrong.

"Oh, son," said he, "look up!"

He saw then three holes in the roof of the palace through each of which the biggest barrel could pass.

"What has happened?" said Iron Waist.

"Three giants came in," said the father. "They just caught the Furious Flame by the shoulders and carried her out through the roof!"

"Didn't I tell you," said Iron Waist, "to stay and look after your wife? You will have to go in search of her tomorrow."

"Where shall I go?" said Terror without Fear.

"You will go to the king," said Iron Waist, "to Fionn Mhac Cumhaill in Gleann Tuirc. All three of them could not have her. They would have to go and get a decision as to which man of them would have her."

Early as the sun rose, Iron Waist arose earlier. He made breakfast for Terror without Fear. "Get up now," said he, "and put on your armor! You will have to go to Gleann Tuirc."

He put on his two curved carved shoes below his two fine Greek graceful greaves plated with Spanish silver. He took up his smooth, shining sword, narrow in front and broad behind, which had an edge for shaving, an edge for cutting, an edge over an edge, and still a third edge, so that if he had been born yesterday, he would have been a strong man today. He did three trial tricks under the open sky. He came down on his right heel. He said to himself, if it is under water or over water, under earth or over earth that his wife should be, that he would surely find her.

He went down to the brink of the beach, he and his comrade Iron Waist. Iron Waist took out a little board of pinewood, and cut a sliver from it, and made a spacious sailing ship. He gave it a shove that sent it a mile out to sea.

"Now, comrade," said he, "give me your pocket knife. I will open it every day while you are away. If rust comes on the knife, I shall follow you, and I shall find you wherever you may be. But go first to Gleann Tuirc."

He said farewell to his comrade Iron Waist. "Take good care of my father and mother until I come back."

"Good-bye now!" said Iron Waist. "And set the sails on her!"

He made a leap from the beach and went on board the ship. He set aloft her great taut and tightening sails to the tops of her masts and left no rope untied, no helm unlashed, no oar unready, the seagulls crying from stem to stern, the sand going down and the foam coming up, out into the deep, deep, desert sea, and he gave her a third and two thirds of sail. With heelabow hollabow the eels arose in wheels together, and the fish of the sea and the birds of the air made fairy music and merriment with joy and pleasure at Terror without Fear going in search of his wife to Gleann Tuirc.

He came to the harbor of Howth, where the first ship was headed and the first warrior landed. He tied her with lines to hold for a year and day, in such a way that no sun could split her and no rock could wreck her, if she were to be there for a thousand years until he should come again.

He took her two anchors and buried them in the beach. He had not gone far up when a warrior came down to meet him.

Terror without Fear

They spoke in the fair fortunate words that were used in those days. The warrior who had come to meet him asked who he was and where he was going.

"There is my name," said he, "on the hilt of my sword, and you may read it."

"Oh," said the warrior, "you are Terror without Fear. You are going in search of your wife!"

"Yes, but tell on," said Terror without Fear. "Where are you going, and what is your own name?"

"I am one of Fionn Mhac Cumhaill's warriors," said he, "and my name is Oscar."

They went up together to the king's house. The king came out, and as soon as he saw Terror without Fear he sent at once for Goll. Goll came before him.

"Where is the wife of Terror without Fear?" said he.

"My mother has charge of her," said Goll, "and she has put me under *geasa* not to approach her for a year and day; and, by dad, I will not part with her until she is taken from me by force."

"Will you fight for her?" said Fionn.

"By dad, I will, master!" said Goll. He called the king out into the courtyard then. "Chew your thumb," said he, "and find out whether you could stop us each evening at six o'clock." Fionn chewed his thumb, and he declared that a truce was to be granted by Terror without Fear every evening. "Well, master," said he, "give us only an egg every morning and another when we stop in the evening."

Goll had a knife called the Big Knife of Goll the Lucky. He

was able to eat enough with it from a single egg each day, however long he should have to fight, until he won the victory.

Next morning at six o'clock they were called in, Goll and Terror without Fear. There were laid on the table before them two eggs, two knives, and two spoons. There was neither bite nor sup to be had by them except an egg apiece until six o'clock in the evening, and then to stop until six the next morning. Goll used to go home then to his mother and sleep in his bed. The harp used to begin to play, and Terror without Fear to dance! So it went on for eight nights and eight days, and it was on the ninth day that Goll killed him.

"Now," said Fionn, "since Terror without Fear is dead, we must bury him fittingly and kindly, with a tombstone over the grave. I am sure that they will come in search of him.

That was the ninth day at twelve o'clock when he was killed. On the morning of the tenth day, when Iron Waist got up, he saw rust on the knife. "Father and Mother," said he, "my brother and comrade is dead!"

Iron Waist was eight feet tall and eight feet broad. He jumped up and put on his armor, a short suit of Indian rubber. He took his sword in hand, and said farewell to the father and mother, and to the cooks and maids and servants of the palace. He told them to do everything that had to be done until he should come back, and that he hoped he would not be long away. He went down to the brink of the beach. He drew out a board of pinewood and made a little boat of it. He put his oars into the water and said to himself that she would overtake the March wind ahead of her seven times, and the March wind astern would not overtake her. Three hours and a half it took until he reached Gleann Tuirc away across the sea.

He saw the ship tied up. "Oh," said he, "you are my comrade's ship!" He tied his boat beside her. "I had better dress myself and make a warrior of myself. Unless I am armed," said he, "my head will fall!"

He put on his short suit of Indian rubber, his two curved carved shoes below his two fine Greek graceful greaves plated with Spanish silver. He took up his smooth, shining sword, which had an edge for shaving, an edge for cutting, an edge over an edge, and still a third edge, so that if he had been born yesterday, he would have been a strong man today. He took his sword and put it on his wrist and twisted the strap nine times around his wrist. He walked up.

Fionn saw him coming. He chewed his thumb at once. He found out from his thumb that unless he could make peace with Iron Waist, he would not leave a head on shoulders of all the Fenians. And the number that was there was twenty-one houses with twenty-one fires on every hearth and twenty-one men around each fire. That was the number of the Fenians that were in Tara of the Hosts at that time.

"Now," said Fionn to the Fenians, "go all of you into hiding until I see what sort of talk Iron Waist will make!" Then he lay down in an infant's cradle. "Now," said he to the maids, "when he comes in, he will ask where the Fenians are. You tell him that we have gone on to the mountain with so many chains and cables. He will ask what for. You tell him that we took a wild boar in the forest yesterday, and that when he was stretched on the ground each of his legs covered five miles. When he is going out," said he, "lay on the dinner table twenty-one oat-cakes baked on griddles three and a half feet wide, twenty-one flasks of beer, and twenty-one haunches of venison."

Iron Waist came in. He asked was that the king's palace. The maids said that it was. He asked where were the Fenians. They told him that they were gone on to the mountain with so many chains and cables.

"Why?" said Iron Waist.

"They took a wild boar in the forest," said they, "and when he was stretched on the ground, each of his legs covered five miles, and they said to themselves that they would have a nice morsel in it when they brought it home."

"Whatever may happen to the boar with his chains and cables, let them all be here to meet me at two o'clock tomorrow!"

When he was going out, two of the maids stopped him. "We have orders from the king not to let any man go without his dinner," they said. "Please sit down!" He sat down. They laid before him on the dinner table twenty-one oat-cakes baked on steel griddles three and a half feet wide, twenty-one flasks of beer, twenty-one haunches of venison. He found the last morsel as sweet as the first. He cleared the whole table.

When he had finished dinner, Fionn began to cry in the cradle. He asked who owned the child. The maids said it was the master's child. "Please put your hand into the cradle," they said, "and rock it for a while." He put down his hand, and while rocking the cradle, he put his finger into the king's mouth. He bit the finger with all the strength of his jaw and could not break the skin.

"How old is the child?" said Iron Waist.

"A year and a half," they said.

"Well, tell the king," said he, "to rear him well till he is twenty-one, and after that he will be a fairly good warrior."

He stood up. He laid a netfull of gold on the table to pay for his dinner. "There are ten thousand pounds there," said he, "and divide it among yourselves to pay for the dinner. But tell your master to be here to meet me at ten o'clock tomorrow with all the Fenians." Then he went off. He went down toward the sea.

The king got out of the cradle. The Fenians all came in at once. "Go," said he to Oscar. "You are the quickest—and bring him up!"

"We have come back from the mountain. Fionn bade me tell you to come along with me." Iron Waist went back.

Fionn shook hands with him. "Well," said he, "when your comrade came in search of his wife, Goll said that he would not part with her unless a man should take her from him by force, since he had held her against the three Sharachauns."

"Where is Goll now?" said Iron Waist.

"I am here," said Goll.

"Well, Goll," said he, "will you fight me?"

"Oh, by dad, I will not!" said Goll.

"You had better not fight him," said Fionn. "Come on,"

said Fionn to Iron Waist, "so that I may show you where your comrade is buried; and I am the man who can bring him back to life."

He took a cup of healing balm and his magic rod. He put a drop of the healing balm in the mouth of Terror without Fear and in his nose and ears. He stood up as strong and active as ever. He asked where Goll was.

"I am here," said Goll.

"Even so," said Iron Waist, "since you could not beat him the first time, you shall not hurt him now."

Terror without Fear said farewell to Fionn Mhac Cumhaill. His wife, the Furious Flame, came to join them. They brought her home. They stayed at home, and the three of them were in and out together for ten years. He made two halves of the land, the cattle and the town, so that Iron Waist could marry, and that is the end of the story of Terror without Fear and his wife, the Furious Flame, daughter of Second Rod without Tidings, and his comrade was Iron Waist.